G R JORDAN

A Sweeping Darkness

Inferno - Book 3

First edition

ISBN: 978-1-915562-26-5

This book was professionally typeset on Reedsy.
Find out more at reedsy.com

True success requires sacrifice.

RICK RIORDAN

Contents

Foreword

The events of this book, while based on known areas in Scotland, are in an entirely fictional setting and all persons are entirely fictitious.

Acknowledgement

To Ken, Jessica, Jean, Colin, Evelyn, John and Rosemary for your work in bringing this novel to completion, your time and effort is deeply appreciated.

Novels by G R Jordan

The Highlands and Islands Detective series (Crime)

1. Water's Edge
2. The Bothy
3. The Horror Weekend
4. The Small Ferry
5. Dead at Third Man
6. The Pirate Club
7. A Personal Agenda
8. A Just Punishment
9. The Numerous Deaths of Santa Claus
10. Our Gated Community
11. The Satchel
12. Culhwch Alpha
13. Fair Market Value
14. The Coach Bomber
15. The Culling at Singing Sands
16. Where Justice Fails
17. The Cortado Club
18. Cleared to Die
19. Man Overboard!
20. Antisocial Behaviour
21. Rogues' Gallery
22. The Death of Macleod - Inferno Book 1

Kirsten Stewart Thrillers (Thriller)

The Contessa Munroe Mysteries (Cozy Mystery)

The Patrick Smythe Series (Crime)

Austerley & Kirkgordon Series (Fantasy)

1. Crescendo!
2. The Darkness at Dillingham
3. Dagon's Revenge
4. Ship of Doom

Supernatural and Elder Threat Assessment Agency (SETAA) Series (Fantasy)

1. Scarlett O'Meara: Beastmaster

Island Adventures Series (Cosy Fantasy Adventure)

1. Surface Tensions

Dark Wen Series (Horror Fantasy)

1. The Blasphemous Welcome
2. The Demon's Chalice

Chapter 01

Macleod swung his legs out of bed and stood up, stretching out with both arms. He felt the shoulder blades tight and somewhat sore, but he started to rotate his arms, first in small circles, then working up to bigger ones. At full circle he stopped and went backwards, tightening them in again until he finished where he'd started with his arms out straight, standing like a live version of the Angel of the North.

Having completed this, Macleod turned and looked down at the face smiling from the bed. Jane lay unashamedly bare, looking at him, smiling up and he felt her warmth. He was about to go back into battle, about to reach into the darkness again, but he needed this, this time alone, this time of being built back up. He hadn't told her anything about the case. He hadn't mentioned Gleary and she'd not asked.

It wasn't over; no, it was far from over. There might even be darker times ahead. He listened to her talking about the markets intently, the bargain she'd picked up, how she'd occupied her time alone and without him. He wasn't worried about her in that sense. Jane was more than capable of looking after herself, handling her time. He was more worried about how the job at times shut him off from her. He would talk to Hope more about it.

He'd recently talked to Clarissa, something he'd never really imagined himself doing, but this one had been tough; this one had stretched him to the maximum and inside his head, he was struggling, struggling with the image of the next child, the next killing. It was coming; he knew it was coming and he had to get there first. It was 6:00 a.m. and Macleod continued in his underpants towards the large window of the bedroom where he drew back the curtains. The dawn wasn't up yet, hadn't even begun, and he peered out into the darkness.

'Do you mind?' said Jane. 'You don't know what sort of perverts are watching the house. We've had news crews here before, remember?'

'I remember,' said Macleod quietly. 'We left and I didn't know if we were going to come back here. When it all blew over, would I want to be here? Would I want to leave Inverness? I've thought about it, Jane. I've thought about it all, quitting.'

'You can't quit,' she said.

'Of course, I can quit. There are always good detectives coming up behind. Hope's going to be a fine one. She had her metal really tested this time, and had to work alongside Lawson. Ross nearly lost his cool at Lawson.'

'Ross nearly lost his cool? Ross doesn't lose his cool with anyone.'

'No, he doesn't, but they got to him this time as well. A child he was adopting, they actually tried to kill that child. I'm sure that was deliberate.'

'It can't have been easy.'

'No, it wasn't. Clarissa saved them—him and the child. Banged up, ready for her pension and she saved them. Who'd

2

have thought it?' asked Macleod 'Who'd have thought Clarissa would come to the rescue?'

'She's sweet on you. Are you aware of that?'

Macleod looked over his shoulder to stare down at Jane. 'You feeling a challenge?'

'I didn't say you were sweet on her. I said she was sweet on you.'

Macleod stared back out of the window contemplating the fact that his middle-aged partner was talking about a crush from an older middle-aged woman on her older middle-aged man. Seemed like the thing teens should be doing or at least newlyweds. Something akin to that age, not Macleod's years. He needed to stop using that word, age. There came a point when you didn't feel what age you were. Maybe age was just irrelevant because the body's going anyway.

'Are you okay, Seoras?' said Jane suddenly. 'You haven't mentioned anything about it, not a thing.'

'I can't with this one,' he said. 'I can't. Well, maybe one day. For now, I can't.'

'Make sure you're talking to someone; you hear me, love? Make sure you're talking to someone.'

'I'll talk to Hope.'

'Not Jona?'

'No, Hope. Hope gets me in a way that Jona doesn't. Jona's different when it comes to things like this. Even with the kids, she's a pathologist. They just see bodies in a different way.'

'I don't think you give her enough credit,' said Jane. 'They're not just bodies to them; they are people. It's why they do it; it's why they try to find out.'

'I know,' said Macleod.

'Can you see anyone out there?' said Jane.

'No,' said Macleod. 'No one at all.'

He heard the creak of the bed and the pad of her footsteps and her arms were around his neck, hugging his body tightly.

'You said you were worried about somebody looking in.'

'It's all right,' she said, 'I can cling nice and tight to you.' And he let her, and they took a moment together just enjoying the embrace.

'Do you think you'll get them?' asked Jane.

'What sort of a question is that? If the press asked that question, I would tell them enquiries are continuing and we were doing our utmost to get them. Arrest the correct criminals, murderers, whatever.'

'Press isn't asking,' said Jane. 'I am. Will you get them?'

'Yes,' said Macleod with determination in him. 'I'll blooming well get them. We have to get them on this one.' He felt her hands squeezing his and she pressed tighter to him again.

'I believe you, Seoras; I trust you. Make sure you do, Inspector, because you won't live with yourself if you don't.'

Macleod had let Jane lie in after that, getting himself a couple of croissants and a black coffee before making the relatively short trip across the Kessock Bridge down to the Inverness Police Station. He sailed into his office just past seven and noted that Ross was already over in the far corner.

'Coffee, sir?'

Macleod stopped. 'What if I said no?' said Macleod.

'I'd take you across to Raigmore hospital, have you examined.'

Macleod gave a smile. 'Coffee please, Ross.'

He walked into his office and sat behind his desk where he looked at some files that were on it and began reading through them. There were reports from Jona, and a message from the

Assistant Chief Constable to contact him at some point this morning so he could run Macleod through the plan he had concocted the previous night as to how the media would be dealt with.

In truth, Macleod couldn't care less. It was all about the case now. All about getting to this group, whatever, whoever they were, before they got to the kids. There was a rap at the door. Macleod, without looking up, called for the person to enter. He saw a coffee cup out of the corner of his eye being placed, but it wasn't placed in the correct spot.

Ross always put it about six inches to the right of him and about four inches forward of where his hands would sit on the desk. This one was wider than that. Someone who wasn't so particular about what they did. *Maybe*, he thought, *maybe they are making me stretch for it, forcing me to look up*.

Without doing so, he said, 'Hope, how are we today?'

'It's good to have you back. I've told everybody to be ready in the next ten minutes. I hope that suits you.'

'Does, indeed,' said Macleod, and reached over, took the cup of coffee and began sipping it. *Yes*, he thought, *Ross made this one*. It was good.

'Are you okay, Seoras?' asked Hope. 'You up for this?'

He glanced up at her, his face determined, and then he returned to his papers.

'Good,' she said. 'Ten minutes.'

Ten minutes later, Ross filed through to sit at the round table in Macleod's office, closely followed by Hope. Approximately a minute later, Macleod saw through the glass in his own office, Clarissa hobbling in and throwing a jacket up on the coat rack. She wasn't wearing a shawl today. It kind of threw him. Then again, it had got completely soaked, and was probably off at the dry cleaners. The shawl, after all, was a work of art, not just some common item you picked up from a clothes shop. The door banged open and Clarissa hobbled through.

'Sorry. Foot's killing me. Had to go and get it taped up before I came in, but I'm fine. Thanks for asking.'

'Sit down, you're a minute late,' said Macleod.

'He's on form, isn't he?' said Clarissa. 'You're certainly on form.'

'Sit down. Look.' Macleod pointed to a piece of paper in the middle of the desk, on which was written an address indicating the Spittal of Glenshee area.

'This came from Gleary. Whatever we think of how he got it, it came from Gleary. He extracted it from his niece, who'd been running the knives. If I know Gleary for the utter sod of a man that he is, he would've extracted this in a harsh fashion. She would've begged to give it up.'

The team looked back up at him silently and then back down to the address.

'I've got problems how we got to here, but here is where we are and that's one of our leads. Ross, Clarissa, you're on that address. We also need to look deeper into the Mackies. We've got two bodies. We've got Sandra Mackay raped and her child killed. She was raped by her twin brother. A violation, albeit one she was almost unaware of. How did the Mackies get to this point? Kyle Mackie's flat needs looked at. I've contacted Jona to do that. Hope and I will chase down the Mackies.'

'Why?' asked Ross. 'I don't understand. We were charging along good lines before. Me and the sergeant, you and Clarissa.'

'Bluntly, Ross. You've got two old farts here that need looking after. One thing I'm very aware of is that all of us have nearly died on this case whether we worked it inside, or on the outside. We try to stick together. You and Hope are the most able-bodied, Ross. You are probably the most able bodied now because of Hope's injury in her arm. She'll look after me. You'll look after Clarissa.'

'I don't need no damn looking after.'

'You complained about your foot when you came in. You almost drowned with me. I don't care how street smart you are, you blooming well need looking after. Okay?'

Clarissa almost jumped back. 'Okay, Seoras. No need to beat my head off.'

'No, sorry, there probably wasn't any need. But we look after each other, and we keep it tight. Okay?'

'Okay,' said Ross. 'Sounds good, and we need to work quick. Remember Kyle Mackie's warning? Killings are coming, more of them. We've been fortunate during recent investigations. Well, fortunate in the sense that no kids have been lost in the recent time frame. Can't say the same about all of the bodies, can we? We've now got an expectation from the public.'

'Ignore it,' spat Macleod, deliberately. 'The Assistant Chief Constable's taking care of the media. We let him take care of it. All of it. You get anyone comes in asking for comment, you fire it to Jim. Jim's going to give us all the backing we need. You get a comment about the former DCI, it goes to Jim. Everything goes to the Assistant Chief Constable. Is that understood?'

There was a general murmur about the table. Macleod knew they didn't need another reminder.

'We have a lead for the knives and we have a couple of dead brothers who have been involved in these killings. We know there's twelve knives and they have been used four times. If you use a separate knife for each killing, that means yet more children are in danger. Let's not forget, he talked about a big event. I really want to know how big an event that is. You're tired, you're exhausted, you're half beaten up. We've been pulled apart on this one, hauled back together. Heads up. Be aware. I don't want anyone walking in solo again and nearly getting killed.

'It was dumb, but we've all been dumb at times on this one. It's time to start being smart. It's time to get there and close it off before even worse happens. You know what we're to do. Does anybody want any further instruction?' There was a general shaking of heads. 'In that case, let's go. Get out there; find what we need.' Macleod watched the team stand, but Hope waited while the others cleared away.

'You okay sending them to that address given what's happened around obtaining it?'

'They can go with police escort if they want,' said Macleod. 'It's not a problem. I'm too close to that address, Hope,' said Macleod suddenly. 'I almost feel responsible for Gleary's niece.'

'Gleary's responsible for his niece. You know that. That's how this works. People who put knives into people, people who kill people, they are responsible, not anyone else.'

'It's an easy thing to say,' Macleod returned. 'It's just too easy to say.'

'Where do we start with the Mackies?' she asked.

'Sandra Mackie. There's only her and her sister alive, and who knows where her sister is?'

Chapter 02

Macleod sat in the passenger seat as Hope drove to Sandra Mackie's home. The two stayed in relative silence. They were never that talkative in the car together. It was one of the things that Macleod always liked travelling with Hope. With Clarissa, you got this constant verbal barrage about something or other. Ross was different again. Always fussing and making sure you're okay and, 'Do you need this, sir? Have you thought about that, sir?' Hope just let him be.

He was also remembering what Jane had said. Clarissa was sweet on him. It wasn't something he wanted to encourage, develop, or in any way saw as a good thing. When he thought back over the previous cases, she was always on the lookout, trying to find a man that would suit her, and he wondered what sort of a man that would be. Why someone like him? He thought he was miserable at times, and he certainly couldn't handle a woman like Clarissa. She never stopped, always charging about here, there, and wherever.

It was the inane babble about pieces of art that got him. Macleod and art had never really sat together. He got the ones with the landscapes, beauty of God's earth and all that.

Somebody had put half a cow in formaldehyde or something like that. Was that art? Hope told him it was art when they spoke about it. Art made you think. He always thought bomb attacks made him think, but he never considered them art.

Hope parked the car close to Sandra Mackie's. When they knocked on the door, it took a while before the woman arrived, pulling the door back slowly. She was in her dressing gown, her hair unkempt. Macleod could see the tears coming and he didn't blame her. After all, she'd lost her child, and well, there was the really messed up part of it, if you could say that, that had also happened with her twin, left him struggling to get his head around it. No wonder she couldn't.

'Sandra,' said Hope, 'I was wondering if we could come in; we need to ask you some questions about your brothers.'

'Which one? In fact, what does it matter which one? They took away my wee one. They took Britney away. How? How do you do that? How do you do that to your niece? How do you . . .'

Hope stepped forward, encouraging the woman to go inside. She was starting to become slightly hysterical, and while Hope and Macleod certainly didn't blame her, these things were best carried out in the privacy of her own home. They didn't want her becoming a freak show.

The news crews and the papers would still be about. They'd certainly take any story on Sandra Mackie. They'd probably be all over her again once they realised that her twin was so deeply involved. Macleod was holding a lot of this close to his chest for this reason.

Macleod put the kettle on while Hope sought out some coffee and tea in the cupboards. Three discovered cups later, Sandra was drinking incredibly thick tea while the other two were drinking what Macleod considered to be greasy-spoon-café-level coffee.

'When was the last time you saw them?' asked Hope.

'You mean before?'

'Yes, before what your brother did.'

'It'd been a few weeks with Kyle,' she said. 'Kyle would be out around the town. Although I never spent any time with him, it wasn't unusual to see him about occasionally. Didn't usually bother though, but I was interested this time because, well, you see, Kyle had a woman on his arm.'

'Can you describe her?'

'Well, she had a figure. She wasn't young but she had a figure. That's the way Kyle liked them though. Big on top.'

Macleod thought if he had made that comment, he would be getting hauled in front of some standards board, being spoken to in how to refer to women of certain sizes. He rarely referred to women in any way except by strict detailed description; it was much safer.

'Kyle was always weird, especially with his magic and that stuff, and he always thought himself above us. Maybe he was right. Look at the state of the rest of us. As for . . .'

'Nathan?' asked Hope.

'I don't want to say his name. I don't want to mention him. How do you do that? He was part of me, my twin. Do you understand it? You probably don't. Do you even have any siblings?'

Macleod shook his head. Hope indicated she didn't either. 'It's okay.' said Hope. 'Just slowly, whatever you can tell us. You were talking about Kyle?'

'Yes, Kyle was with a woman, as I said. Good looking woman, big on top and she seemed reasonably enamoured with him, which I thought was quite strange.'

'Did you catch a name for her?' asked Macleod.

'He called her Karen, and she worked at a DIY store. One of those large ones where all the would-be punters go. Where you go to screw up a house before you get a proper person in to sort it out. One of those places. She looked nice and I didn't think anything of it. I wished them all the best back then. She realised that Kyle thought he was above us, so I can understand if he killed Nathan for what he did. Justice.'

'What else did Kyle get up to? In the past—anything in specific?' asked Macleod.

'Not really. He was a bit of a loner. Like I say, he always thought he was above the rest of us. He did start writing to other people though. He was big into his pen friends' idea. I think that was good for Kyle. People would be aloof, you could prepare the answers before you wrote to them. Find out a bit more before you have to engage properly.'

'Do you think any of these friends influenced him at all?'

'Well, he used to be very keen on one person amongst the pen pals. Guy by the name of Sammy. That was right, Sammy. That's where Kyle got his interest. Like I say, the occult and all that stuff. Kyle liked to tell everyone he's a magician and the powers were coming from elsewhere, not some sort of an illusion.'

'Yes, I got the same story,' said Hope. 'Even when Ross made it obvious that we didn't think you'd need powers.'

'He used to talk about powers, wanting them, telling you how cool it would be. "Can you imagine," he used to say to me, "walk down the street and if somebody calls you out or has a go at you, I'd click the fingers and down they drop."'

'That's pretty macabre,' said Hope.

'Well, Kyle always was macabre.'

'Do you think he still has any of that correspondence?' asked Macleod.

'I've no idea,' said Sandra. 'He never showed it to me. I'd say he learned all his magic in it because that's where the interest grew when this pen pal exchange went on, but I never saw any of it. He never wanted to show it to anyone which I thought was fair enough. He wasn't that old. Why would you want everything exposed, put out in front of everyone, especially from a faraway friend? It's not somebody that's going to come to your rescue, is it?'

'By any chance,' said Macleod, 'can you remember what the boy's second name was that he wrote to?'

'Sammy something. Sammy Tarbs. Sammy Tarbs. No, no, no, no, no. Forbsey. Sammy Forbes. That's right. He called him Forbsey once. Sammy Forbes.'

Hope shot a look across at Macleod that Sandra picked up on.

'What's up? Why do you ask that?'

'It could be important to the enquiry,' said Macleod. 'I can't say yet for definite but there's a strong possibility. Have you taken up any counselling?' he asked.

'Well, they said they're going to offer it.'

'I think you should. You've been through a lot. Incredibly unpleasant. If I was you I'd take every bit of help I can get.'

They spent another twenty minutes with Sandra before making their way out back to the car and sitting down for a conference.

'She's doing remarkably well,' said Macleod. 'I'm surprised she hasn't gone and jumped off a bridge. It's been gross what's happened to her?'

'You think we should check this Karen out then?'

'DIY stores,' said Macleod. 'You go do them and I'll go and talk to Mr. Forbes.'

'It might be a difficult one.'

'No,' said Macleod. 'Every time we go near Forbes, from what you've told me and what I've seen, he edges away. The key thing here is to flush him out. Make him move. Like I said, I'll see him and I'll sort him. Don't worry, but you need to find the Karen. Drop me off back at the station. I'll take my own car then.'

As the car made its way back to the Inverness Police Station, Hope reached over and put her hand upon Macleod's knee. 'I did miss you. He tried to bribe me into jumping into your shoes. Stick with me. That's what he kept telling me. He kept telling me that if I wanted to go places, all I had to do was get on track with him.'

'How did you read him?' asked Macleod. 'I was talking to Jim last night and he asked me if I thought the DCI was involved.'

'We didn't find any connection,' said Hope.

'No,' said Macleod. 'But that's not what I'm asking you. What do you think?'

Hope considered and then she shook her head. 'I think we need more evidence because if he's playing the part of the fool, he played it darn well, but it's good to have you back, Seoras.' She tapped his knee again. 'I was getting kind of sick of this incompetent man. He kept leering at me all the time.'

'Well, I can't really chastise him too heavily for that one,' said Macleod. 'There was a time.'

'That's long gone,' said Hope. 'But you don't look all right. What's the matter?'

'Did you get a look in any of the papers? '

'No,' said Hope. 'Why?'

'A whole big spread. Macleod's back on the case. It's like World War One. We're going to jump over there, a jolly good show, and I'll get back for tea and medals. That's the way the press are speaking about us. Oh, and you'd hate the photo.'

'Why,' she said.

'Well, I look pretty bad because I'm just getting out of a car in a raincoat. I don't know when they took it, but it's a full-length shot of you.'

'Why would I hate that?'

'Well, on the cheaper ones, it's kind of blowing up so half your rear end's in the photo.'

She laughed. 'If that's what they're reduced to now to sell newspapers, Lord help us.'

'Do you want to take somebody with you,' said Macleod, 'when you go around these DIY stores?'

'No. No, I don't.'

The car continued in the middle of the silence until they parked up at the police station, but as Macleod went to get out of the car, Hope put her hand on his shoulder.

'Under the water, having to breathe through a hole. Are you okay? Are you going to be able to continue? Nobody's going to bat an eyelid if you don't go through with this one, or have trouble with it.'

'You're not kicking me off the case to take it for yourself,' said Macleod and watched her laugh before her face grew serious again.

'That was a serious incident. Just don't get too obsessed about our safety,' said Hope. 'You and Clarissa have been through the worst. Get some help on that and we'll do all right. How long do you think we've got, by the way?'

'Who knows?' said Macleod. 'It could be tomorrow, it could be the next day, it could be a week, a month, six months from now. How long does it take to kidnap that number of kids, hold them, and then bring them all together?'

'Let's hope it's plenty of days,' said Hope. 'If we're lucky, we might just catch them.'

'Luck's got nothing to do with it,' said Macleod. 'You take the Karens and I'll take Forbes.'

'Just beware. He might be a wily character.'

'As I remember it, if I can get past his wife, I'll be all right.'

Chapter 03

The drive to Spittal of Glenshee in the small green sports car was done in relative silence. Ross felt comfortable again. The boss was back, and for that, he was truly glad. He wasn't one to kick off a fuss, wasn't one to be impertinent or shake the tree, but he had found DCI Lawson almost impossible to work with. Neither had Ross appreciated when he got the investigation dumped on him when Hope had been put in hospital to recover from her escapade in the river.

Now that Macleod was back along with Clarissa, they could focus on solving this case. As Ross had known, Macleod had come up with something, yet he also saw an uneasiness in the boss, and he wondered just how much it had cost the man to find out the information he had done while he'd been removed from the case. Beside him, Clarissa said nothing about the previous investigations, except when it had been mentioned about how they had fared and why she had a new shawl.

Clarissa had said their time on the outside had been generally rough. The shawl, unfortunately, had suffered an irreparable tear. That was clearly a lie, thought Ross, for a woman who loved that shawl, something had happened, but she was sporting a new one, this time in a tartan. She hadn't brought it upstairs to the office though and maybe she hadn't wanted a discussion about what had happened to the old one. Ross believed it was Urquhart tartan, but he wasn't that good on the various patterns. He thought about asking her for more information but then decided against it.

Climbing into the Cairngorms, they arrived at the address, an abandoned farm located amongst a sparse collection of buildings. The village, if it could be called that, was on a highland road, tight into the mountains. It probably was an excellent tourist route in the summer. Today, however, there was a grey mist hanging over, rain was falling, and Ross felt the cold. Once outside the car, he put on his gloves as well as a black beanie hat, about the most he thought he could get away with while still looking like a proper police officer.

If he hadn't used it, his ears would have frozen. Ross always thought that the Scottish weather was at its worst when it was cold and raining. The cold was bad enough, the wind sending a chill through you, but when it rained with it, it added an extra dimension, freezing you to the bone even when the rain stopped. You were now wet, and the cold didn't stop seeping through.

The farm building was a rather small affair and as far as Ross could see, hadn't been used in a long time. Inside, there was no furniture and several of the white walls had plaster flaking off them where mildew and dampness had got the better of the structure. Several windows were cracked, and Ross struggled to see that anyone would be living here.

'Looks like a dead end from the boss, doesn't it?' said Clarissa. 'All of that for this.'

'Do you think it's a false lead? Someone set us up again?'

'I'm not sure,' said Clarissa. 'Last time you wanted to

investigate, the place looked lived in, looked like a possibility. This looks like an abandoned wreck.'

'Maybe it's just where they pick the stuff up from. Maybe it's not meant to be somewhere lived in.'

'It's well out of the way,' said Clarissa.

'You could drive up.'

'Risky,' she said. 'Whoever dropped it off, if they didn't know you, could wait and see the car come. You would want to be watching it, wouldn't you?' she said. 'Make sure you were clear.'

'You think somebody was up here? Like camping out in the woods.'

'Possibly. But there's got to be other ways to do it.'

'Well,' said Ross, 'why don't we have a look around the nearby accommodation? I mean, there may be something. Pickup couldn't have been that long ago. We'd have been out of summer season heading into the winter. Maybe there wouldn't have been that many people up here.'

'It's a good call,' said Clarissa. 'Come on, jump back in the car. Do you think they do those big log fires up here? I could really do with one.'

'Maybe you should get a car with a proper heating system,' said Ross.

'You leave my car alone! You say another word like that, you'll walk back.'

Ross saw the cheeky smile, got back inside the passenger side of the car and Clarissa drove them around the local area. There wasn't much within a mile except for a guest house which hadn't had anybody within the last three months because they'd been doing the place up.

Climbing further into the Cairngorms, they spotted a hotel

approximately three-quarters of a mile from the farm. The driveway was stone, and as they got up to the top where the hotel sat on the hill, Ross could see a large waterfall behind it.

'That's pretty stunning,' he said. 'Isn't it?'

'Still cold,' said Clarissa. 'Come on, let's see what they've got.'

The hotel was what would have been described as a house hotel. Not a large grand building, but a rather smaller affair. Ross reckoned they could only have had about ten or twelve rooms. That being said, the carpet was plush. A large wooden fixture provided the reception counter and Ross could see a large brass bell waiting to be rung. Clarissa picked it up and rang it like she was a town crier, which meant the sound echoed through the small corridors. A rather efficient bald man suddenly appeared, dressed in a tartan waistcoat.

'That's enough to wake the dead. I was only in the next room.'

'Sorry,' said Ross. 'She gets excited.'

The man looked over at Clarissa, gave a smile at her shawl. 'Urquhart, is it?' he said. 'Nice. Very nice. Looks like proper quality material with it.'

'Of course, it's quality material,' said Clarissa, and spun slightly, allowing the man to see her shawl.

'Well, how can I help you fine people?'

Ross saw the man look at him quizzically. They were rather an odd combination. The younger Ross with the older Clarissa, her purple hair, rather crazy, and the loud shawl alongside his neat suit.

'I'm Detective Constable Alan Ross,' he said, pulling out his warrant card. 'This is Detective Sergeant Clarissa Urquhart. I'm sorry to disturb you, sir. We're just carrying out some investigations and would like to know who you've had staying over the past month.'

'Well,' he said, 'that's the register there in front of you. You're welcome to take a copy of that. How else I can help you? Is there anybody you're looking for in particular?'

'Do you know the farm about three-quarter miles down the road?' asked Ross.

'Of course, Glentwine Farm, or as it was. Been abandoned now maybe fifteen years. He found it hard to make a go but he stuck at it until he was seventy-five, at which point he died. The son's never really bothered since.'

'Glentwine? A bit of an unusual name.'

'Unusual people. He had some sort of strange hobby.'

'In what way?' asked Ross.

'He sometimes would make coffins. He wasn't an undertaker but he had a collection. I remember being down there in my younger day, asking him what was in the barn and he took me in and showed me excellently made coffins. Don't get me wrong; they were good coffins, if you're into that kind of thing.'

'Who's into that sort of thing?' asked Clarissa.

'Well, I'd have thought undertakers, someone like that,' said the man. 'You see that's the thing. He never actually used them. They were just . . . well . . .'

'What?' asked Ross.

'He was into all that vampire lore and that as well. Bit of a strange one.'

'Was he married?' asked Ross.

'He had been. She left him, but that was some ten years before I saw those coffins. People had said she was just fed up with them. I think there was more than that.'

'Is she about?'

'No,' he said, 'Morag died six years after leaving him. There were no kids either, in case you were wondering.'

'What happened to her?' asked Ross.

'She died in a skiing accident, from what I gathered. She left him and found some young lad. They went off skiing and the two of them went down the wrong slope. Pist you call it, isn't it? Apparently far too high a category for them. Took a wrong turn and sailed off the end of it to a rather large drop. Certainly, too large for them to survive it. Tragic, really. She deserved a lot better than that.'

'He died when?'

'Let's see. I think it was ten or fifteen years ago. The place has been abandoned since.'

'Did anybody ever buy it?' asked Ross.

The man shook his head and put his hand to his chin thoughtfully. 'Not that I'm aware of. Would have heard about that sort of thing. It's just sat there. I'm not sure anybody even dealt with his affairs to be honest. Like I said, no kids. Maybe he would've had brothers, although I can't remember any, or sisters. Then maybe he was that strange that they didn't bother.'

'What about the funeral?' asked Clarissa.

'Well, there was one done for him, buried him in the local cemetery. To be honest, I'm not sure he would've wanted that. There was a joke around here. He got up the next night—ran off somewhere else.'

'Not a church person then.'

'No, he wasn't.'

'Anybody been asking about that place?' queried Ross.

'Maybe it was a month ago, month and a half. We had a gentleman up here. He came up in the kilt and that, but I didn't buy it.'

'Didn't buy what?' asked Ross.

'He didn't buy the fact that he was Scottish,' said Clarissa. 'There's a lot of us wear the tartan but, as you know, Ross, we just wear it. This shawl, it's just part of who I am. The gentleman here in his trews and his waistcoat, part of running the business. I suspect outside you maybe wear a kilt, too.'

'It's easier in the trews during the day, but yes. I wear the kilt a lot for walking.'

'This man,' said Ross, 'you reckon he was just what? Having it on for a laugh?'

'He came up with the deerstalker hat and he had a tweed jacket and a kilt, but it was Stewart Tartan. It wasn't any particular family but the one that anyone gets to wear as a subject of the monarch. A lot of the tourists wear that, which is fair enough, I guess. He asked me specifically, "How do you get down to the farm?" Pointed it out on the map to me but didn't seem to know the name of it. He wasn't local. Stayed here for five nights I think and went out with a backpack every day. For four days, the backpack was empty when he came back. Wasn't really full when he left either. Fifth day, backpack was full. I found it a bit strange but he paid his bill and then left. He was nice enough to talk to. One of those people though who didn't tell you anything about himself. Just asked about you. If it hadn't have been for the backpack, I wouldn't have thought anything of it. Some people are like that.'

'How did he pay?' asked Clarissa. 'A card at all?'

'Cash,' said the man. 'Everything was paid for in cash. Had a reasonable bit of it from what I could see.'

'Car?'

'No,' said the man. 'Arrived in a taxi, got me to get him a taxi out of here down to the train station.'

'He came up here with all his refinery,' said Ross. 'Goes out walking every day in a backpack that never got filled until one day he came back with a full one. Took a taxi here. What was his name?'

'Alexander. Let's have a look. Alexander Stollin.'

'Did he show you any credentials at all?' asked Ross. 'Driving license, passport, for that?'

'Cash up front, so no, didn't bother. Quite happy with that.'

'What'd he look like?' asked Clarissa. 'Any pictures?'

The man pulled his phone out. 'I do, actually. I was with the missus outside and since the day was braw, we decided to take one of those selfies that you do with the camera. We don't post much on the social media but I decided that this was worth it. I'm standing there, in my trews and my waistcoat and that. She's out looking lovely beside me. I got photobombed by this guy. Not that he meant to.'

The man placed his phone down in the work surface and Ross looked at it. There was the photograph of the hotel proprietor with his wife. Their faces encompassed at least three quarters of the image but the other quarter had a man standing upright. Ross tried to blow the picture up on the phone. He was struggling to place the face.

'Can you send me that?' said Ross. 'If you don't mind? We won't use anything of you but I wish to identify that man.'

'Of course. Not a problem.' Ross waited by the man as he tapped on his phone and then saw the image arrive to the email address that Ross had given him.

'Is there anything else I can do for you?' he said, 'I've got to get on. We need to get into town, pick up some of the local groceries. We might not look busy but there's a small party coming up in the next couple of days. Got to feed them

24

somehow.'

'Of course,' said Ross, 'I won't take up any more of your time.'

There was a cough from Clarissa. 'I don't suppose you've got a log fire, do you?'

'I do indeed, Sergeant. If you go through those doors in front of you, you can sit down and have a seat.'

'Any chance of coffee?' she asked. 'I'm absolutely frozen. I'll pay for it, of course.'

'I'll be right through with it,' said the man. 'I take it. You'll be having one as well, constable?'

'She's the boss,' said Ross. 'So, I guess so.'

Chapter 04

H ope sat in the car looking at her phone with a smile on her face. The last while had been rough, especially with Macleod out of the picture but now he was back. She felt the team was itself again. He called in the troops, discussed, and then sent them out and now they were on the trail.

Inverness had a number of DIY stores and she had phoned the local staff to find out if anyone called Karen worked there. There were two. One at a smaller concern near the industrial estate, and the other at one of the largest DIY retailers in the country. Hope scooted around to the smaller concern first and found herself looking hard for management. This was due to the fact that the place seemed busy but mainly with tradesmen and Hope ended up walking to the manager's office and banging on their door.

As it opened, she felt a blast of heat coming from inside. She didn't blame him for being warm in his office, for the warehouse had a cold chill about it, but his face looked like thunder.

'What's up?'

'I'm sorry, I was looking for some of your staff but . . .'

'Joan, who's in?' asked the manager to someone.

'Ian.'

'Where the hell are you?'

'No, no, no,' said Hope, 'I don't want to be a bother.'

'It's no bother,' he said in a friendly face. 'You're far from the worst interruption I've had today and you're a customer, so we'll gladly help you.'

'I'm not a customer,' said Hope. 'I'm actually here on business. Detective Sergeant Hope McGrath.' The warrant card came out and the man studied it carefully.

'What do you want with me?' he asked.

'I don't want anything with you,' Hope replied. 'Do you have a Karen working here?'

'Karen, yes I do,' he said. 'In fact, I'll take you to her if you want.'

'Please,' said Hope, and fell in behind the man as he started to weave his way through the warehouse. Eventually, he turned down a paint aisle and pointed all the way to the bottom.

'That's Karen Armstrong—been working with us for a number of years.'

Hope looked at her. The woman was in her sixties and seemed to be busily efficient, tidying away paint pots.

'Karen,' said the man, 'come here a minute.' The woman walked up, smiled at Hope, and then looked at her boss. 'The police want a word with you,' he said.

'With me? What have I done?'

'I don't know if you've done anything, ma'am. I'm detective Sergeant Hope McGrath. I just wanted to know if you knew Kyle Mackie.'

'No,' she said. 'Never heard of him.'

Hope looked at the woman and tried to match her with the

27

description Ross had given when he'd seen the woman arrive at Kyle Mackie's house. It was clear the woman wasn't the right person, so Hope drove to the next DIY store, the national chain. On arrival, she was taken by a man at the front door to the boss's office which was up a set of metal steps on a gantry that looked out across a vast warehouse.

The door opened, and Hope found herself looking at a woman in her fifties. At first, she thought, *that's strange*, and then she corrected herself from what she considered to be a very chauvinistic attitude. *Of course, women can do this job. We can do any job. Why am I looking surprised? Maybe it's because she's actually got the job.* The woman behind the desk barely looked up, shuffled some papers before she gave a grunt and said, 'Yes?'

'Detective Sergeant Hope McGrath. I require your assistance, Miss?'

'Mrs Armstrong,' she said. 'I'm the manager of this place. How can I help you?'

'I want to know if you employ a Karen.'

'Karen? Possibly. Hang on a minute.'

The woman pressed a little intercom, and a secretary came in from the next office. 'Susan, we got a Karen on the books?'

'Yes, Karen Wicklow. Been here for six months.'

'What age is she roughly?' asked Hope.

'Thirties, forties. Something like that.'

'Would you mind if I go to meet her?'

'Is she in?' asked Mrs Armstrong.

'She is indeed in today,' said the secretary. 'I'll take you to her, detective.'

Hope found herself ushered out of the office quickly, and the secretary took her to a woman dressed in overalls in the gardening section of the store.

'Karen, this is Detective Sergeant McGrath. She wishes to speak to you.'

The woman looked around quickly, Hope thought, *almost startled.*

'Sorry to bother you,' said Hope, 'but I could do with a word. Is there anywhere we can go?'

'You can take her upstairs,' said the secretary. 'One of the spare offices. There's nobody in them at the moment.'

Karen nodded, and without saying a word, led Hope back towards the main office before cutting off and entering another room, high up in the gantry area.

'Sorry about the officiousness of it,' said Karen once in the room. 'You can have a chair if you want. What's this all about?'

'Karen, would you know a Kyle Mackie?'

'Why?'

'Answer the question first, please,' said Hope. 'Do you know a Kyle Mackie? It's just that someone fitting your description was seen with him recently.'

Hope noticed the wedding ring on the woman's finger. 'You can tell me,' said Hope. 'I can be discreet.'

'I don't earn much money here,' said Karen. 'Sometimes I take on some other jobs. You have to understand my husband; he works offshore and he doesn't exactly give me much money. I have this job for my own and well, I do something when I want a little bit extra.'

'What do you do, Karen?'

The woman blushed for a moment and then she shook her head almost proudly. Hope thought she stood like a peacock.

'I'm an escort,' she said. 'I do rather well from it.'

'Did Kyle Mackie hire you as an escort?'

29

'Kyle has hired me a number of times,' she said. 'From what I have gathered, he's quite a recluse. He's the magician guy.'

'That's right,' said Hope. 'Unfortunately, he's now a dead magician.'

The woman looked shocked, reeled backwards, and sat down on a chair. 'That's a bit of a blow.'

'I imagine it is. When did you last see him?'

'A week or so ago. I think. Maybe not even that. Took a bottle of wine around to him. Kyle paid for certain things.'

'You stay the night?' asked Hope.

'I did. Left the next morning.'

At least that side of the story tallies, thought Hope. She was still feeling rather uneasy about the woman. 'So, what can you tell me about Kyle Mackie?'

'Not a lot. I'm there to listen if they want to talk or if they don't, I'm there to do other things. Mr. Mackie wanted to do lots of other things.'

'Did he ever ask you to do anything weird?'

'Weird? He did strap me up on a spinning wheel once and threw knives at me. That was weird.'

'Did he do it blindfolded?' asked Hope.

'No,' she said. 'I think I might have freaked out at that point. He would have me dress up in an assistant's outfit, as he called it. That's not what we would call it in the business. More of a customer entertainment outfit.'

Hope nodded, and she saw the woman sit forward now, more comfortable and relaxed. She seemed to be getting over the man's death rather quickly. 'I'll need you to make a full statement just because the man died,' said Hope. 'Would you like to come down with me now?'

'No,' said the woman. 'See, the escort work actually isn't

known by my husband. In fact, it's not known at all, so the last thing I want to do is to have that brought up. I'm quite happy to make a statement, but if we can keep it quiet as much as possible.'

'Of course,' said Hope. 'When would you like to do it?'

'If tomorrow's not a problem,' said Karen, 'we can do it then.'

'I was hoping to get it done today,' said Hope.

'I'm working and then my husband will be home. Not a great idea. Don't want to explain why I have to go.'

'He's not on the rig at the moment?'

'No,' she said. 'He's sitting at home.'

'Well, tomorrow then,' said Hope. She took out her card and handed it over to the woman. 'Make sure you give me a call, let me know when you're coming in, but please tomorrow at the latest.' Hope shook the woman's hand and found herself escorted by Karen to the front door of the building.

Hope walked off and got to her car but noted that Karen was still watching. After turning on the ignition, Hope drove out of the car park, spun around the block, and drove back in, parking in a different spot. She sat and watched the doors of the building and began to count. When she'd reached eight hundred and fifty-three, she saw Karen step out of the building.

Karen took a quick look around the car park and Hope ducked down behind the wheel. When she next looked up, Karen's car was leaving, and Hope started her own and began to follow. Hope tailed the woman back to a small house on a terrace in the old town. Parking up a distance from it, Hope kept watching as the woman first went in, then came out with a suitcase.

She threw it into the boot of the car and drove off out of Inverness. Soon she turned up to a nearby village and found a small hotel. It was one that would have maybe twenty rooms in it and looked rather dilapidated. Maybe they did the coach parties as that came through. That was always a winner. Sandwiches and soup, charging the earth for it, no doubt.

Once the woman had checked in, Hope approached the front desk and rang the bell inside. The hotel didn't look any better inside than outside, and she saw wallpaper that was slowly making its way off the wall trying to form an overhang. There was mould up in the cornice as well, and the carpet had several threadbare bits. An older man dressed rather scruffily approached reception and give Hope the once over.

'Tell me you're looking for a room,' he said. Then she heard a voice from the back.

'Ian, is that a customer?'

'Don't worry, Love, I've got it,' said Ian quickly, and again gave Hope another once over. His mouth hung open, half chewing, which reminded Hope of a salivating dog.

'I'm sorry to bother you,' said Hope. 'I was wondering if my friend was staying here as I'm looking to surprise her. You see, it's her birthday and her family knew she'd come up these parts, but we didn't know where she was staying. Would it be possible to have a look at your register?'

'You can look at anything you want here,' said the man and continue to stand, chewing.

'Where is it?' asked Hope.

'Right here. Come around this side and I'll show you.' The man opened a book and Hope rather innocently walked around to the other side.

She was going to be able to examine whatever she wanted, and the last thing she needed to do was to tell him she was police, worried in case he passed it on to Karen at some point.

She stood scanning the names and Hope felt a hand on her backside. If any other man had done it she would have turned around and brained him, but she needed to stay in character at this point.

'Is there another page?'

'Yes,' said the man. 'That's yesterday you're looking at.' His hand hadn't moved from her bottom, and if anything, he was leaning in closer. His breath was foul.

She stepped back from the book once she saw the most recent entry. *Tanya Jones*. Karen was already using an alias. Hope went to step away from the book, but found a rather strong hand holding her in position. The man was slightly smaller than her and was now leaning around towards her front in a position that Hope found incredibly lecherous.

'Ian, are you coming in here? I need some help.'

'Busy at the moment, Love,' said Ian, almost chortling.

'He's just helping me,' said Hope loudly. The woman came through the door like a flash. Hope wasn't sure if Ian had managed to get his hand off her backside without the woman seeing.

'I just needed to see if my friend was staying, but I've seen it now and she's not. I'll not trouble you any further.'

'I don't think you should; sorry, your friend's not here,' said the woman. 'Off you go.'

Hope almost laughed as she walked out the door. She gave a glance back, seeing the man get a rather large clip around the ear from his wife. *Sod deserved it*, she thought. *Unbelievable*. But she'd got in and out with the name that Karen was using as an alias without being discovered. Karen was going to be worth watching. Hope went out to the car and sat down, pondering her next move.

Chapter 05

Macleod was feeling an enjoyable familiarity with what was going on. The team were out hunting down clues, interviewing suspects, and though the situation was tense with the potential of more killings, it was like he was back in the old seat again. Sitting in the passenger side of his car, he looked across at the young female constable who had been grabbed to drive him about today. It wasn't that Macleod couldn't drive himself, but he thought with the recent past, the number of dangers they'd faced, it would be best if there were at least two of them.

He wasn't so worried about Hope. After all, she was just searching through some DIY stores, but he was going to interview Samuel Forbes, potentially part of the group. Forbes's wife had given everyone the heave-ho last time, but Macleod was more determined now, for the man seemed to be a key figure. He'd known Kyle Mackie had been a pen-friend to him, and Macleod wondered how long that friendship had continued. Had it still been in the mix until recently?

One thing he thought about the group that was perpetrating the killings was that they weren't shy about removing their own. It made him think there was a greater purpose at work here. It reminded him of serial killers when they got to the point of seeing their plans go awry. Certain things were important; certain things couldn't be compromised. To have a group of people focused like that did not bode well.

Often, though, there was a key player who wasn't so focused, someone who struggled to have that fervour, like they were along for the ride and then all of a sudden, the ride got too busy, got too rough. Some people had limits, but nobody was running out of the woodwork just now.

Macleod sat and wondered what it would be like to be in a group that instructed each other on how to carve symbols into the backs and fronts of children. He tried to wander into the minds, something that was normal practice for him, but he didn't understand how you could do that and then sit in an office or maybe teach at a school or whatever their job was, as if everything was normal. But then, that was their normal, wasn't it?

He was trying not to make it personal as well, but he felt the call to solve this. The upside-down crosses were on the front of the children. More than that, they were a direct challenge.

In his professional life, Macleod had always separated his faith from his police work. There was the law to follow; there was the law that would convict, the law that would be upheld. Sometimes his faith and the law didn't match up. He remembered traveling to talk to the one who got away. His faith demanded that he let her know what she'd done and to give her a chance at redemption. The law had nothing to say to her.

Here, the law had a lot to say. You didn't get to kill children, but there was more than simple murder to mark them like that. It was almost like a curse, one he'd have to eradicate. He'd gone

35

beyond the lines to stop them. He'd gone to a place that he didn't want to be in. A place that made him feel compromised, gave him unsavoury thoughts. The fate of Gleary's niece still hung around in the back of his head. Could he have done that differently? If he had, would it have worked out or would he just have had more dead children on his hands? It was funny how sometimes he felt he didn't want his faith. It demanded too much.

'We're here, Inspector,' said the young woman beside him, and Macleod nodded.

'I'm not sure I recognise you. Have you been in long?'

'No, Inspector. Only been on the force about a year. Not long transferred up to Inverness.'

'Nice place to live. I came up from Glasgow. Seen a few things though.'

'Yes, Inspector. It's well known. They talk about you quite a bit.'

'Well, don't let them tell you anything. What's your name, by the way?' asked Macleod.

'Constable Rippon.'

'I'm Detective Inspector Macleod, but nowadays, we go by the first names. I'm Seoras. You can call me Seoras, unless we're in front of the public, in which case sometimes it's better to be a bit more formal.'

'Okay, Seoras,' said the woman, but Macleod could see her hands were shaking. 'I'm Louise.'

'Well, thank you for driving me up. When we go to interview, let me take the questions. You're here for my safety.' The woman looked over at him, almost nervous. 'I said to the sergeant, "You owe me someone who can handle themselves if something kicked off." He said you could.'

'Yes, Seoras, I can handle it. I box.'

'Women's boxing?' said Macleod. 'I used to have a constable who was into mixed martial arts. She's gone onto many other things. Forgive me, but I just found it a bit weird. I guess the martial arts is all new to me. Boxing was always around, and it was always men. You any good?'

'I'm still working in the police force,' said Louise. 'Guess I'm not that good.'

Macleod laughed and opened the car door. 'You'll do,' he said, 'you'll do. Now, game face on.'

Together they walked up the short driveway and Macleod rang the doorbell of the rather neat house. They heard a momentary kerfuffle behind the door, possibly because someone was looking out of a peephole. Then the door opened to reveal Samuel Forbes, who stared at Macleod intently.

'I hope you've got good reason to be here, Inspector.'

'I've always got good reason to be wherever I am. I need to ask you some questions, Forbes. I can do it here or we can go down the station. It's in regard to a murder inquiry.'

'Well, I guess you can do it here.' Forbes was looking around him, maybe wondering if any neighbours were peering out.

'Do you know the name Kyle Mackie?'

Forbes retreated back about three inches, rocking on his heels as if the question had struck a blow against him.

'It's a name from the past, Inspector. There used to be a Kyle Mackie that was one of my pen-friends back in the day. It's a long time ago, though.'

'What was the relationship with Mr Mackie?' asked Macleod.

'Like I said, we were pen-friends. Typical boys writing back and forward about this and that. There wasn't really much

37

else in it.'

'How did it come about?' asked Macleod.

'Well, with similar interests and that.'

'From what I know about Kyle Mackie,' said Macleod, 'his interests included the occult.'

'Really? I wasn't deeply into the occult then. I obviously have a more academic interest in it now,' said Forbes, 'but Kyle was certainly into magic, but he seemed to think it was real. I mean, there comes a point in your life when you understand that the magicians are just illusionists, don't you? You don't believe all that stuff. It's a bit like going to church, isn't it?'

Macleod felt a twang inside but he maintained his composure.

'How do you mean?' asked Macleod.

'Well, when you go to Sunday school, they feed you all that stuff. It's all fairy tales, isn't it, Inspector?'

'Not everyone thinks that,' said Macleod. 'Some people, they like to look on the other side of the fairy tale.'

'But it's all sweetness and light, isn't it? That's the thing about the church, isn't it? All sweetness and light. Very dark on the other side. It's not what you would call pure.'

'People are rarely pure,' said Macleod.

'Are you a believer? Is it constable?'

'The only thing I believe,' said Constable Rippon, 'is that the inspector is asking you a question.'

'Well trained, isn't she?' said Forbes.

'Never mind that,' said Macleod. 'What happened with your relationship with Kyle Mackie?'

'Well, like I say, he seemed to think it was real. Started to get very fanciful. Just lost touch. Didn't feel like it was worth talking to him. How's he doing anyway?'

'Badly,' said Macleod. 'He got murdered. Possibly by some people that had lost the faith.'

'Dreadful,' said Forbes. 'Absolutely dreadful.'

'What happened to the letters that you wrote to each other?'

'I threw them all out,' he said.

'That's interesting,' said Macleod. 'He didn't.' There was a moment's silence as Forbes tried to outstare Macleod, but the inspector held his gaze, and the smallest of smiles came across his lips. 'Somebody tried to shut him up. It seems to be their ploy. Somebody's out of line and if we get close to them, somebody shuts them up. The thing is that just killing somebody doesn't shut them up. There are too many other things in a person's life. Too many other things in their life that speak. Simply killing someone doesn't end what they're trying to say.'

'Well, that sounds a little bit complicated for me, Inspector,' said Forbes.

'Who's at the door?' said a voice. Macleod recognised Forbes's wife. She appeared beside Forbes dressed in smart trousers and a blouse, with a face that looked like thunder. 'What are you doing here?'

'I'm asking your husband some questions, so I don't have to take him downtown and ask him there.'

'What? About who?'

'About a certain Kyle Mackie.' Macleod watched the woman's face, but she seemed completely unaware of who the man was.

'Was he a student or something? How are you meant to know him?'

'He's from your husband's past. Old pen-friend. Never mentioned it, did he?'

39

'Why would I mention it? It's a pen-friend from the past,' said Forbes.

'Just wondered if you're into the same sort of things.'

'They let you back on the case then, Inspector?' said Mrs Forbes. 'I'm surprised at that. You made a cock-up before, didn't you? That's why they took you away.'

Macleod stared at her, then glanced back towards Forbes. He didn't want to get distracted by this woman.

'You need to get back to chasing real criminals. Stop annoying my husband. Go on, off with you. Off with you.'

'I'm afraid that's not how it works,' said Macleod, 'and for your information, I didn't screw up, and if you've watched the news, you'd know that, instead of just taking the gossip here and there. I was right all along and I'm still right. Sometimes you must have faith. You have to keep going.'

'Sometimes the faith takes you places you don't want to go,' said Forbes, 'I guess.'

He knows, thought Macleod. *He knows and I can't get a hold of him for now, but there's also a woman involved. I also think there's a woman in the group. Mrs Forbes looks ideal for it. She's like his Rottweiler. Same as Clarissa is for me, chasing off the enemy.*

'Well, I'll leave you in peace,' said Macleod. 'If you find any of that correspondence you had from earlier years, do drop it in to us. Just trying to understand the mind of Kyle Mackie, if you understand where I'm coming from.'

'Indeed,' said Forbes. 'It's a pity the poor man's dead.'

'Well, there's nothing of the dead around here,' said Mrs Forbes. 'Begone, Inspector.'

Macleod tipped his head forward. 'Good day. I hope you have a pleasant one. Be thinking of you.' He turned and walked back to the car hearing constable Rippon's footsteps beside him. When they slid inside and began to drive away, Rippon looked over at him.

'Can I ask a question, Seoras?'

'Of course, Louise.'

'That was a bit strange. All that talk of faith and stuff. What was that about?'

'That was about a man who knows a lot more than what he's letting on. That I do know, but what did you make of the woman? Does she know more than she's letting on?'

'If she does,' said Louise, 'she's not letting you know it. There's nothing there to suggest that she knew Kyle Mackie.'

'You think her reaction was genuine when she looked surprised?'

'Surprised?' queried Louise. 'I wouldn't have said surprised. I'd have said just nonplussed as if who was that.'

'I think you're right,' said Macleod. 'You could well be right, Louise. Now back to the station.'

'Coffee?'

'Life doesn't revolve around coffee,' and he saw Louise quickly whip her head back to the road looking out the front of the car. 'But,' he said, 'it should be a companion on the journey.' He watched the woman laugh. Any bit of humour just to break the dark feelings he had inside him.

Chapter 06

Ross sat behind his desk, glaring at the screen in front of him when he saw Macleod re-enter the office. He gave a wave and Ross jumped up ready to reach for the coffee. A constable was following Macleod into the office, and with a quick shake of his hand, Ross was instructed to sit back down and he watched as the young woman made her way over to the coffee machine. She picked up two cups and began to pour them.

'That's not the Inspector's cup. Two to the right, that's the Inspector's. He'll want it in that cup.'

'Ross will want it in that cup,' said a voice from the office. Macleod was watching at the door. 'They try and tell you how fussy I am, how I like this, and I like that. It's not me, it's them.'

'Of course, sir,' said Ross. He did the coffee. He felt a little bit agitated and looked over at the young constable. 'Louise, isn't it?' he said.

'Yes. I'm sorry. I don't know your name.'

'I'm Ross.'

'Ross who?' she asked.

'Just Ross. Always Ross. The Inspector takes it black. Nothing in it. You see the blend on the side. It's always that one. We don't put anything else in this machine.'

'Noted,' she said. 'I doubt I'll be making the coffee for that long. Just here to drive him about.'

'You any good on computers?' asked Ross.

'Not overly,' she said. 'Most of my job's been manning the line during riots or protests, parades, things like that. Basic duties with house visits. Haven't really done much detective work.'

Ross felt less threatened and sat back down on his chair, staring at the screen in front of him. There was a photograph there, a selfie taken by a couple from a hotel near Spittal of Glenshee, and at the back of the photograph was a man who had gone to the house where the knives had been sent to.

Ross was trying to make the image clearer. As he did so, he thought the man had at some point had some work done on his nose. It didn't look cosmetic, more work carried out by an unhappy party. It was almost as if it had been smashed in at some point.

He clicked on the computer and sent a copy of the photo over to his boss's phone. Hope was out at the moment, and he wasn't sure when he'd get a reply, but he wondered if the man was who had run across at them when they'd gone to the golf club and saved his potential adopted child. Ross was still shaking from that and seeing the man's face gave him shivers. But Ross hadn't clocked him clearly. Hope, having sent Ross on ahead towards the child, had tackled the man. At least she'd know if it were he. The sergeant would be able to advise.

Clarissa Urquhart strode into the room, tentatively putting her new shawl up on the coat stand, before spotting the constable pouring the coffee.

'Is she allowed to do that?' asked Clarissa.

'Well, I don't think it's really . . .' started Ross, but he was interrupted as a voice shouted from the small office at the top of the room.

'Leave her alone. She's making me coffee. Just let her bring it in.'

Ross saw Louise turn and suddenly, she seemed slightly taken aback by the woman in front of her.

'You're Sergeant Urquhart, aren't you?'

'That's right, and who are you touching the inspector's coffee?'

'Leave her alone.'

'The inspector just asked for some coffee. Seoras said he wanted coffee.'

'Seoras?' said Clarissa. 'Seoras said that?' Ross saw Louise look beyond Clarissa, almost for help, and Macleod appeared behind her.

'Yes, Seoras asked for coffee. Now, would the two of you leave the poor girl alone and let her come into my office with the coffee? I've got work to do.'

'Nice to meet you,' said Louise to Clarissa. 'I've heard a lot about you, Sergeant Urquhart.'

'It's Clarissa,' said Macleod. 'Don't let her intimidate you.'

'They call you . . .' began Louise.

'Don't believe all that either,' interrupted Macleod. 'Will you just bring the coffee into the office?'

'Yes, sir.'

'It's Seoras,' said Macleod, and he looked over at Ross briefly. 'Are you getting anywhere?'

'Possibly, sir, but I'm waiting for the sergeant to get back to me. Possible ID on who collected the knives.'

'Good. Anything else?'

'No, sir.'

'Good, Ross. Let me know as soon as.' Macleod turned on his heel. Louise looked over at Ross. 'You can call him Seoras.'

Clarissa laughed. 'Don't go there,' she said. 'Just don't go there.' Louise disappeared with two cups of coffee into the small office and Ross sat back in his chair.

'Heard from her yet?' asked Clarissa.

'No, I don't know what she's doing though. She hasn't checked in for a while.'

'I'm surprised he let her go out on her own. Especially after that talk earlier.'

'She's only going to DIY stores,' said Ross. 'It's hardly anything dangerous.'

'More like he thinks she can handle it. Not me. I have my knight in shining armour here to look after me.'

'I don't think that's funny,' said Ross. 'We nearly lost her. Nearly lost you too. Nearly lost my child.'

Clarissa popped onto the edge of a desk, her shoulders slumping. 'Yes. Probably best not to keep thinking about that,' she said. 'Best to just get on, yes?'

Ross nodded. 'It'll come. Don't worry. It'll come. At least the little nipper's safe.'

Ross stood up, walked to the machine and poured two coffees, handing Clarissa one. By the time he'd sat back in a seat, he'd heard a ping from his phone. He looked down at the message.

Same guy we saw on the golf course. The one I had the scuffle with. Possibly could have been the one who knifed me. Don't know his name but we need to find out.

Ross read the message through twice and looked up at Clarissa. 'Got a hit. It's the guy that jumped the sergeant down at the golf course before you and the boss arrived.'

'So definitely part of the circle,' said Clarissa. 'You've got to put that photo out then.'

'Hang on,' said Ross, and he stood up, marched over to the small office door, knocked it before pushing it open. 'Sorry to interrupt, sir.'

'It's okay,' said Macleod. 'What's up?'

'Just heard back from the sergeant. It seems the man who went to the house where the knives were and collected them, is the same man that attacked myself and the sergeant on the golf course before I managed to save Daniel. He could possibly be the guy who killed Kyle Mackie and knifed the sergeant.'

'Do we know who he is?'

'No idea,' said Ross. 'Can I circulate it around the force?'

'You can circulate it wherever you want.' Then Macleod stopped. 'Circulate it on the quiet. Around the force. Don't say what it's in connection with, just keep it low key.'

Suddenly, a waft of purple hair appeared over Ross' shoulder. 'Can I send it other places?'

Ross could feel Clarissa's hand on his shoulder, leaning on him. He wasn't sure if it was because of her foot and the pain she still felt from it, or if she was trying to appear in a comical fashion. Either way, she was hurting his shoulder.

'Where do you want to send it?' asked Macleod.

'Well,' she said, 'I'd like to send it around the art world. This seems to be the guy who was sent to pick up the knives, organised a drop possibly. Some people may have seen him. He may have reached out to acquire the knives in the first place. I mean, look at him. With a smashed-up nose, you're not going to forget him, are you?'

'Well, that's true,' said Macleod, and he sat back, took his cup, and began to sip his coffee.

'Thinking it over,' Clarissa whispered in Ross's ear. 'He's thinking it over. He's going to go for it. He's going to go for it, Al's.'

Ross just wanted to turn round and tell her to get off his shoulder. Clarissa wasn't an extremely large woman, but she was no delicate waif either, and Ross reckoned she was only standing on one leg, putting most of her weight onto him. He wished the boss would decide quickly.

Macleod took the cup down from his mouth, set it on the table, and looked over at Constable Rippon. 'What do you reckon, Louise? I mean I'm not asking whether Ross should send it out to the force. Quite happy with that. What about sending it out to the art world?'

'I don't understand all of the case,' said Louise, 'but as I gather, these people are not afraid to tidy up, so to speak. If they think someone's been compromised, they just kill them. There's an extreme risk of that.'

'She's right, Clarissa,' said Macleod, firing the question back over to his sergeant.

'It's a calculated risk. We haven't got a lot, Seoras. We need a lot more. We need to act, and we need to act quickly,' said Clarissa. 'Yes, he could end up dead, but we could also get more information quickly and we may also find him. The long and the short of it is we need to find someone in this group and find out what's happening with these killings. With the potential large event coming up, I don't think we can afford not to.'

'I didn't know about the large event coming up,' said Louise. 'What's that?'

'Need to know,' said Macleod. 'If you get more involved in

the case, I'll bring you up to speed. But Clarissa is right. You see, they call her my Rottweiler but she's more than a fancy pair of teeth.'

'Charmed,' said Clarissa. 'I'll just get on with it then.'

'Get off Ross's shoulder,' said Macleod. 'You're half-killing him.'

'Were you making faces?' said Clarissa to Ross and gave him a shove on the shoulder before half-limping back into the office.

'Get on it,' said Macleod to Ross. 'See if we can get a hit quickly. Where's Hope, by the way?'

'Not sure. The sergeant replied to me about the photo, but she hasn't checked in about where she is. I can give her a ring if you want.'

'I can give her a ring,' said Macleod. 'It's fine, Ross. Give Clarissa a hand if she needs it. Not good with the technology, Louise, you see.'

Ross turned, walked back out of the office and straight into Clarissa who was asking him the easiest way to send out a picture to all her contacts. Ross spent the next twenty minutes making the message happen. Once he was satisfied that Clarissa had sent it out properly, he began to circulate the photograph around the rest of the force. He then spent the next hour and a half trying to see if he could get a better image of the man, but the picture, while good enough for a human eye, didn't lend itself to being easily matched.

It was after he popped down for a quick bun from the canteen that Ross walked back into the office to see Clarissa in a foul mood.

'Are you all right?' he said.

'No,' she said. 'I've got a hit.'

'A hit on what?'

'The image. I put it out to my contacts, and someone's come back saying that they've been with that person, whoever they are.'

'And?'

'Well, this person isn't going to want to just fill in a form and send it into us. They deal in some rather dark stuff.'

'So?'

'I'm going to have to go see them.'

'Do I get my coat?' asked Ross.

'Let's just say that she and I don't get on. Not sure how reliable a contact she's going to be either.'

'Have you run it past him?' asked Ross.

'Yes.'

'And?'

'He told me to go.'

'So, let's go,' said Ross. Clarissa hauled herself up onto her good foot, limped across and put her shawl around her. 'Why are you so reluctant?' asked Ross.

'When you get to my age,' said Clarissa, 'you think you've got a certain gravitas. I had that in the art world. I may not have had the looks I once had, but I had the gravitas. Everybody knew that I was on top of it. I was the go-to person. Makes you feel good. Then in walks this girl who looks like you did when you were twenty years younger.' She saw Ross look around. 'Okay, thirty years younger. Worse than that, you can handle the good-looking ones because generally, they're as dense as anything.' Ross raised his eyebrows. 'See, when they come up looking like Lusardi on heat and they've got a mind that matches your own, it's just not fair,' said Clarissa. 'It's just not fair.'

'Let's go,' said Ross. 'Come on.' He let the sergeant hop her way out of the office in front of him. *Who the heck's Lusardi?* thought Ross.

Chapter 07

Macleod spent the late afternoon fretting over what to do. Mrs Forbes bothered him. Constable Rippon said that she felt the woman was genuine. Macleod wasn't so sure; there was something nagging at him and he understood the only way to get past that nag would be to tail the woman in question. He gave a call downstairs for Louise Rippon to come back up to his office and he saw her looking somewhat jaded as she walked in.

'How do you fancy some overtime?'

'I do have plans this evening,' she said. 'Is this necessary? I don't want to disappoint you, sir.'

'You don't disappoint me. I asked you if you wanted some overtime. You can say no, and it's Seoras, remember? Just because you're giving me the answer I don't want, doesn't mean you have to call me sir.'

'Yes. Sorry, Seoras. No, I've got things to do.'

'If you were on this team, it wouldn't work like that,' said Seoras. 'We attend as a team, once we start, that's it. Our better halves have to understand that too. I'm quite fortunate. My partner does, Hope's as well, Ross's. Clarissa doesn't have anyone.'

'You're telling me I should stay?'

'No,' said Macleod. 'I'm just saying that if you ever want to be part of one of these units, that's what to expect. No, go. You've done well today. Thank you.'

He thought that the woman looked slightly disappointed as she left the room and he wondered whether his comment was in any way justified. He just wanted her to understand. People often liked the glamour of the detective role. The constant work was something that she needed to understand. He hoped she hadn't thought he was trying to force her to stay on.

He looked outside to the empty office. There were a couple of constables working, trolling through bits and pieces for Ross, but they too would soon be heading home. *Forget it*, he thought. *It's Mrs Forbes we're tailing. I can do this on my own.*

Macleod stood up, walked over to his coat rack, threw on his long coat and descended the stairs to the rear car park of Inverness Police Station. He should have started to tail her earlier, but he drove out to the Forbes's house. Driving past, he recognised both cars and parked up a little along the street. Macleod sat watching with the radio on until an article came on regarding the killings.

He stuck with it briefly until they started discussing the man on the case. Now that Macleod was back, surely it would be okay. He'd find them. It was awful sitting there hearing yourself talked about especially as he knew that cases didn't always work like that. He wanted to get to the killer in the end, have justice served, but one of the key things was to make sure that he prevented more murders from happening. That possibility was currently far from the case, and he knew with the amount of evidence they had, they were going to struggle. As soon as that happened, the mood of the press and the public might turn. He couldn't concern himself with that though.

About six o'clock, the Forbeses left their house, Samuel taking his wife out by car to a hotel close to the centre. Macleod knew it well because he couldn't afford the dinner in there. He'd taken Jane there once on a very special occasion. She had enjoyed it, but she told him not to do it again. The money that was being asked for the food was something she said she couldn't justify. He found himself agreeing with her very quickly.

Mrs Forbes stepped out of the car and Samuel Forbes drove off. Macleod thought Forbes would simply park up, for there were plenty of spaces, but he didn't. Macleod located himself with a view of the main restaurant. He sat watching as Mrs Forbes was seated at a table and a large glass of wine arrived. It was twenty-five minutes before she was joined by a man. The man was stocky, younger than her, maybe ten years or so, and in good shape. He was certainly paying her plenty of attention. There were little touches of hands across the table, glimpses giving away the feelings that one had for the other.

After the meal concluded, he watched as the gentleman helped her out of her seat and they walked from the restaurant, his hand around her waist. Macleod moved as swiftly as he could from the car to the door of the hotel where he saw them take an access card for a room. They got into the lift, and he glanced through the door as he entered the lobby, seeing them press floor five.

Macleod struggled over to the stairs, attempted to bound up them but found himself struggling by floor three and was almost out of breath when he reached floor five. Peering out of the door, he heard the *bing* of the lift and watched as the couple exited.

They turned away from his end of the corridor, thankfully, and he could see the hands moving from their sides to their backsides and back up again, along with the occasional kiss. Macleod followed them down the corridor until they entered a room, outside which he patrolled for the next fifteen minutes. He then heard signs that confirmed what was happening and he suspected they might be a while before they were back down to the lobby, if indeed they did come down. When he returned to reception, he spoke to the lady behind the desk asking who was in Room 524.

She frowned but Macleod flashed his warrant card and she looked a little bemused. He saw that the name of the man, at least in the book, was Alan Jones. It sounded very much like an alias. There was no one else in the room with him according to the computer. It was almost eleven o'clock when Macleod saw Mrs Forbes exiting the hotel, hurrying over to a cab. Macleod raced over, placing himself in front of the cab's door.

'I think we could do with a word,' said Macleod.

'Inspector? I told you before we don't need to.'

'You're having an affair, and I'm quite impressed how you got him to drive you out to the hotel. Meeting a girlfriend, were you?'

'He's not back in tonight anyway. He said he'd be out.'

'My constable said you were genuine, genuinely concerned for your husband, that you didn't believe anything was up with him. I think we need to chat, Mrs Forbes.'

Macleod turned and opened the door of the taxi, pulled out a twenty-pound note, handed it to the driver and apologised for his time. The taxi drove off and Macleod pointed back inside the hotel. He went to the receptionist, flashed his warrant card again, and asked if there was anywhere he and the lady could sit out of the way. The receptionist looked inside the restaurant, which was now clear, advised they could go to the table at the far end, which would be out of sight of the main window. Macleod nodded, thanked her, and asked for a couple of coffees if that wouldn't be too much trouble. He pointed over to the table and Mrs. Forbes reluctantly made her way over. As she sat down, she looked across at him.

'Are you blackmailing me to find out about my husband?'

'No,' said Macleod. 'I won't tell him about the affair. I'm not interested in your affair; I'm interested in your husband. Understand, I am investigating the deaths of several children and several adults. I think your husband may be involved. He has quite a taste for the occult, doesn't he?'

The woman studied Macleod carefully. 'Don't tell him about this. I'm almost out. I'm almost away. He's got very strange in his old age. When we started off, he was interested in me. Yes, he had quite a thing for the occult and weird tales and that sort of thing, which was fine. I didn't see anything wrong in it, but it's got deeper and deeper within him. You get older and things in the bedroom change. When he has wanted that side of things, he's been very strange.'

'In what way?' asked Macleod.

'He gave me a white monk's habit to wear. Can you believe it?'

'Why you?'

'That's what I thought. It wouldn't have fitted him. To be honest, he didn't really do anything with it. I put it on, he commented, and then he took it off me. It was all a bit bizarre.'

'Anything else?'

'There was the really weird one. He gave me a sheer gown to wear. Now, don't get me wrong, Inspector. When he did

55

that, I thought maybe the interest was rekindling from him, even if it was only in a very carnal way. Then he produced this headwear. That's the best way I can describe it.'

'What do you mean?' asked Macleod.

'He gave me this headpiece. It had antlers coming out of it; had me wear it with the gown.'

'Describe it.'

'Like I said, there were antlers. They looked real as well. Not that I can particularly tell, but they didn't feel like plastic.'

'What did he want you to do?'

'First of all, he had me stand up in it and parade around. I had to walk and it was like he wasn't looking at me. He was more looking at the outfit. Then he had me lie down in it. When I lay down, he said to put my arms out, my legs out, like I would have been strapped. Except he didn't.'

'What did he do after that?'

'After that, I had to undress, and we got on with the sex side of things. The daft thing was the length of the gown was too short for me. The shoulders were tight. It was like something that somebody smaller should be wearing. Someone about five or six inches smaller than me. I told him not to bring it again, especially the headwear. What was that all about? I told him I didn't want any of his occult nonsense when we were trying to make love. He said that wouldn't be a problem because they weren't actually for the bedroom. He just wanted to see how they fitted. We haven't been very close lately.'

'When he gets out and about, do you know where he goes?'

'No. The last five, six years, no. Even before that.'

'Did you know Kyle Mackie?'

'No, not at all,' she answered.

'If I said your husband had been with a large group of men,

would that surprise you?'

'No. He's been to occult meetings before. Daft stuff. Just boys at play really.'

'Look, Mrs Forbes, I'm not one who condones any cheating, but you might have done yourself a favour with this one. Please don't tell him that I've spoken to you.'

'Am I at risk, Inspector?'

'I don't think so.'

'How do you know?'

'The only people that have been at risk have been single women with children. The children have been at risk. Of the women, one died by accident. Anybody that's got in his way, or their way because I don't know if your husband has actually done any of this, they have suffered. Just carry on and get out if you can convince this other man.'

Macleod watched her stand and then she sat down, tears falling from her eyes. 'Do you think he's capable of that?'

'In my line of work, you realise what people are capable of, and it would shock you. He might be, but I need to know he is. Don't talk to him about this. Tell him you had a good time with your girlfriend.'

'Like I said, he'll be late in tonight, and I'll be asleep; then, I'll be out to the gym first thing tomorrow morning. Then, I'll keep out of his way. I wish you had told me sooner. I could have pressed the matter with my man.'

'Yes, tell him Alan Jones is a pathetic cover.'

'His last one was Ignatius. Ignatius Boulder. What he lacks in imagination, he makes up for in general attention. We all need attention, don't we?'

'We do,' said Macleod. He stood up, walked over to the reception, and asked them to call a taxi before escorting Mrs

Forbes to it when it arrived. Macleod handed her a card.

'Keep that safe. Keep it hidden from him. If at any time, you fear for yourself, ring it; we'll come get you. In honest truth, I don't think he's interested in you in that way.'

'Story of my life, Inspector. He's not interested me in any other way either.'

Macleod watched the woman disappearing in the taxi and felt a sadness for her. He thought of Jane at home. She was always waiting for him, accepted the way he was with his work. He realised he was extremely blessed. He shrugged his shoulders and walked back to the car, thinking he might actually go home now. She wouldn't be up; she'd be in bed. She'd hear him get in; she might reach over and cuddle him before he disappeared at six in the morning. He turned on the car ignition, heard the engine spring to life. Then his phone vibrated in his pocket with an SMS message.

Seoras, Hope. I've been tailing one of our Karens from the DIY store. She's in the woods and Samuel Forbes has just turned up.

Chapter 08

It was close to midnight when Clarissa turned the small green sports car off the A9 towards Aviemore. She was looking for the new development, smart posh flats for those young and going well in the world. They would be far too modern for her. Better with a quaint cottage, something with a bit of class to it. Not this vulgar monstrosity that she'd come to. Ross sat quietly in the passenger seat, thoughtful as ever, but he said nothing as she parked the car.

'See those flats? That there is what happens when you give money to people with no taste. They build these things and people with no taste go inside them.'

'It's just a set of flats,' said Ross.

'It's not just a set of flats. This is Aviemore. You want a bit more class than that. Look at the mountains around you. This deserves something with a bit more feel to it. Something more in keeping with the landscape. Something that strikes you as vast.'

'They're flats for people to live in. It's not a prairie land for crops.'

Clarissa looked over at Ross. She swore he was becoming more argumentative.

'It's probably best if I go up and see her. It'll probably just be a distraction.'

'Whatever you think's best,' he said. 'I'll keep an eye here. I don't think we were tailed on the way down.'

Clarissa hadn't thought about that. Then again, why would they be tailed? With the people they were pursuing though, anything might have been possible. Maybe Ross was right.

Clarissa opened the door of the little green sports car, swung her legs out, and hobbled over to where a large pad indicated several different flats. She scanned the names before coming to Scarlet. The Scarlet Woman, that's what they called this one. Good reason too, although it wasn't because of her looseness around men. It was because of her surname. Abby Scarlet. Although the other handle fitted as well.

Clarissa pressed the button and got no response. She pressed it again three times before a voice came back. 'Is it you?'

'It's me,' said Clarissa. 'That's the fourth push.'

'Sorry, music's a bit loud up here.'

Clarissa couldn't hear anything. 'But you did hear the buzzer, though,' she replied and pushed open the door. She climbed three flights of stairs until arriving at the single flat that occupied the third floor. Hobbling over to the door, Clarissa knocked on it and awaited Abby to open it.

Clarissa hauled herself up, trying to stand and look as best as she could, and then wondered why, before the door opened. This wasn't a competition. The woman wasn't in her league. The door swept back and a brunette woman in leather trousers and a low-cut top smiled at Clarissa.

'Been a while. Are you still on that side of the game?'

'You still not appreciating the art? Just making money off it.'

The woman chortled. 'We can trade insults all you want, but

you were the one who came to me, so I thought you'd be a little bit more polite.'

'You thought wrong,' said Clarissa, and marched into the flat.

'You still hold yourself well for an older woman.'

'And you still look like a tart.'

'Well, men seem to like it.'

'Only those without class,' said Clarissa. She looked around the flat, which had a kitchen area as part of its open plan. A leather sofa sat in front of a TV and in the far corner, Clarissa could see a small art collection. She walked over, trying to hold her bearing and not limp, but failed. She accidentally kicked her toe into the wooden flooring and fought not to swear.

'Hurt yourself?' asked Abby and glided past her towards the collection Clarissa was making her way to.

The pictures on the wall seemed brutal to Clarissa. The scenes they depicted on many occasions of torture, pillage, and other grossness from years gone by. Some was clearly fantasy art with scantily clad women wielding swords in outfits that could never survive a fight. Beside them stood impossibly muscly men with loincloths that would need to be secured well for certain parts of the anatomy not to be seen during battle.

'You still enjoy all that stuff?' asked Clarissa, and Abby walked past her pointing to one particular picture. The lack of clothing was apparent, but more than that, Clarissa recognised the face and the figure.

'Who did that one for you?'

'Mons. He's good, isn't he?'

'You've certainly got a fertile imagination,' said Clarissa. 'You've never looked that good.'

Abby put a hand on her shoulder and leaned around. 'Still in denial about me?' Clarissa tutted and the woman stalked off in her high heels towards the kitchen. 'I take it you'll want a coffee, or do you want something stronger?'

'I'm on duty.'

'You don't mind if I do, do you?' Clarissa was left looking at the artwork while Abby made a coffee and then opened a bottle of wine. After taking Clarissa's coffee to her, she collected a glass of wine and strode over to the windows, looking down.

'That's one thing I always did like about you. The hair I couldn't get, the tartan, the shawls. Way older than me,' said Abby. 'You know what? I still like that sports car. I could see myself in it.'

'You have to treat something gently, not abuse it, when it's a piece of class like that,' said Clarissa.

'And a man down there too,' said Abby. She reached over and picked up a pair of binoculars before looking down at the car again. 'Wow,' she said, 'Now that is a piece of class. I could dig him.'

'I'm not sure Constable Ross would dig you,' said Clarissa.

'I think with a little encouragement.'

'I don't think you've got the right sort of encouragement,' said Clarissa. 'But enough of this. It's now gone midnight and I need some answers. The photograph we sent through—where did you know the man from?'

Abby turned and then lay down on her sofa, indicating Clarissa should sit down too.

'You've never forgiven me, have you?' said Abby. 'Because you couldn't catch me. Do you want to see it?'

'You know I'm a policewoman on duty. You know I can just arrest you.'

'You won't. And by the time they come to look for it, it won't be here anyway. I mean, what are you going to do? Attack me? Hold me?'

'I want to know about the man in the photograph.'

'I brought it back, you see. It's hiding. Press a button, that wall comes down and you can see it.'

Clarissa bit her lip. Abby was referring to when Clarissa had investigated her, looking to retrieve a Montrel. It was high-fantasy artwork but worth a packet and Clarissa had realised that Abby had it. She couldn't prove it. For two weeks they had danced around each other, Abby constantly teasing her.

'The man,' said Clarissa, 'in the photograph.'

'Came out of the blue. Turned up at this very door asking about the Knives of Gog.'

'The what?' blurted Clarissa.

'The Knives of Gog.'

'What are the Knives of Gog?'

'You know your Bible, don't you?' asked Abby.

'Apocalypse. The end times. Gog and Magog. Yes, but never heard of the Knives of Gog.'

'I'm not surprised you didn't really follow through on a lot of the more ridiculous superstitions and tales. If you go back into the dark ages, it's there. The monastery at St. Etienne held the history of the world. It's a little-known book. Hasn't got much credence for many scholars. Not that many scholars nowadays know about it,' said Abby. 'But I've seen it and I've read it.'

'Boohoo,' said Clarissa. 'So what?'

'The Knives of Gog, it says that if you sacrifice the innocent and you do it in a certain way and you carve the right things onto them, that basically you can give him a gateway back to the world that will send a pestilence and an evil amongst us to last several thousand years. It's like an anti-Revelation. The one where the devil wins.'

'There's been plenty of that though, hasn't there?'

'It's true, but it's also not well known and it's certainly not well accepted. General academia won't touch it. In fact, most of them won't even know it exists. As an ancient manuscript, it's now no longer in the abbey. I think Russel Carton's got it.'

Clarissa looked up. 'The Australian, the one that lives in Austria?'

'That's him.'

'He's a crack job, total nutter. He goes after anything. Doesn't know a genuine piece in front of his face.'

'I didn't say what he did or didn't know,' said Abby. 'You've got to stop judging people. Start looking at the motives. I make my money because I know what people want. I know how it takes them, how it grabs them. Russell Carton entertained somebody called Forbes not that long ago,' said Abby.

'But how have you read it?'

'Because Russell Carton entertained me once. He wasn't looking for anything of an antique nature. Probably why he didn't have you along.'

'That's very droll,' said Clarissa.

The woman smiled. 'He was entertaining me for purely physical reasons but that's where people don't get me.' She sat up, put her glass of wine down, walked across to what looked like a blank piece of the wall, and pressed it. The wall sprang forward and from the hollow behind, she took out a plastic file containing a number of pages. 'This is the proof, so to speak, that the manuscript exists.'

'You tore the pieces out?' asked Clarissa. 'You tore the pieces out from that book?'

'Pieces fell out,' said Abby. 'I'm not a Philistine. I'd have taken the whole book, but this seemed easier. I'm not even sure he knows it's disappeared.'

'But somebody's obviously read it.'

'He's got the whole thing scanned, translated, written down. If you look at it,' said Abby, 'it's all there.'

Clarissa looked at the pages, worn bits of parchment, and she could see where they would've been bound together. The language in front of her looked like obscure symbols.

'I can't read this,' she said.

'Of course, you can't. They called it demonic something or other. I had to go to the Abbey of Moritz to find a translation, but it confirms the superstition, the idea that the Knives of Gog, when used against the innocent, will bring and wreck terrible vengeance on the land.' Abby reached down and grabbed her wine glass. 'Let's hope you can stop that one, eh?' She took a large gulp.

'Do you believe this stuff?'

'No,' said Abby. 'I don't. It's just writings in an old book.'

'But you're telling me that somebody's got a load of knives and wants to kill children?'

'The Bible could be said to be a load of writings in an old book. A lot of people believe it. A lot of people misinterpret it. Lots of things been done in the name of God and through the Bible, that He might not have been too happy about. Why wouldn't people on the other side do something for theirs?'

'But the Knives of Gog that it alludes to, were they not superstition, too?'

'I think they were,' said Abby. 'I think they were but in 1261, a set was recorded as being used by a number of dark worshippers on the continent. It was north of what was then Turkey's capital. Who knows what they were doing there? There is a trace through to the present day of this set of knives recorded in a history little known. I think it's fake. In fact, no, I know it's fake.'

'But,' said Clarissa.

'A certain Australian had a copy of it, and you put two and two together and people will come up with eight. They won't check that those numbers are right to begin with.'

'You're telling me . . .'

'I'm telling you that somebody can't do their history properly, doesn't check their facts and now actually believes they're going to bring about the return of their own evil master by killing off lots and lots of children. That's how it appears to me. Of course, I might be wrong. You might just have simple lunatics on your hands.'

'Do you mind if I take this?' asked Clarissa.

'Of course, I mind if you take it,' said Abby suddenly. 'I nicked that; he doesn't know I've got it.'

'What about the man with the nose? Did you help him find the knives?'

'No,' said Abby. 'I know what you think of me, Urquhart. I know you think I'm trash. Maybe I'm a bit loose around men. Maybe I don't have your eye for the subtleties of the art. Maybe I focus on money all the time, but I'm not an idiot. Somebody coming looking for knives, knives that were purported to be for the sacrifice and ritual marking of children. There's a lot of things I might stoop to but that is far from anything that I would get involved in.'

'I might need to contact you again,' said Clarissa .

'Well, if it's to do with this, fine. Anything I can do to help.

If it's about anything beyond that, forget it. You work on the wrong side of the fence.'

Clarissa walked over, extended her hand to Abby. 'I don't work in the art world anymore. I'm on totally different fences now. You got me good last time, but I knew you'd done it.' Clarissa extended her hand and Abby shook it. 'You'd make a hell of an investigator,' said Clarissa. 'If I was still on the art team, I'd even tried to recruit you.'

'And how exactly would the police force pay for my tastes?'

'When all you can do is satisfy your tastes,' said Clarissa, 'you'll always come up empty. Thank you.'

As Clarissa went out of the door to take the stairs, still trying not to limp, she heard Abby call after her.

'Next time why don't you bring that Constable Ross up?'

'Definitely,' said Clarissa. 'Definitely.' She would look forward to seeing Abby try and conquer her friend.

Chapter 09

Hope watched as Karen left the hotel in her car. It caused Hope to jolt as she had started to drift off, wondering if the woman would ever leave but then she engaged into full detective mode, eyes wide open, dropping back a nominal distance with the car. As she departed out into the wilds, Hope continued to tail her until she turned into a wood where Hope parked a little distance away.

Quickly she ran through the wood and saw Karen walking down a path heading away from the roadside. Hope continued to remain at a distance, feeling the cold through her leather jacket, but wondering where the woman was going as she hunkered down. After Karen had stopped, Hope watched the woman standing around waiting. She was dressed in just a jumper and jeans which Hope thought was a little bit light considering how cold the nights were getting. As they waited, Hope saw a pair of car headlights turn into the car park. A car door opened and someone got out carrying a large bag. It was a man.

As he got closer, Hope saw him produce a torch, shining it on Karen. She ran up to him, threw her arms around, kissing him long and deeply before he told her they didn't have that much time. Hope recognised the voice of Samuel Forbes. As she knelt, she saw Forbes produce what looked like a white monk's habit and some sort of gown, although it looked very flimsy for the current conditions. Hope watched as Karen stripped down before putting on the gown and gave only a brief shiver. Forbes removed his clothing too, dressing only in the monk's habit. Then Hope sent a text message to Macleod, advising him that the two had met, and where to meet her.

As Hope continued to watch, the pair in front of her became extremely lewd, and yet knives were produced. She watched as they seemed to lay out seven different positions, points they would stand in and practice different knife strokes. They'd also copulate in different ways. It reminded Hope of one of those old Hammer House movies but this was gross, lacking the finesse as if it was being carried out not for a film audience, but for something else. Something that would appreciate the vulgarity.

Hope continued to watch as the pair made their way around each of the seven positions. From her discreet position, Hope tried to clock the knives to see if there was anything recognisable about them but in truth, the only light was the torch that Forbes had provided. Hope also wondered about stepping forward, arresting the pair. After all there had at least been lewd behaviour, but she was only one and they had knives.

She was also worried that if she brought them in, they would be eliminated from the group and the team would be no further on. It was probably better to watch them, to try and tail them, work out where they would go next. After all, Karen was in a hotel unaware that Hope knew where she was. Forbes was also unaware that he was being watched. Now she'd wait until

Macleod got here, then maybe they'd make a move.

It was the best part of half an hour before the gross act in front of her was completed and Hope could see them starting to pack up. She texted Macleod to see where he was and he advised that he was just a few minutes out, so Hope told him she would hold tight. She messaged to see if she should she stop them, but there was no response.

In her head, she had the idea that if the team could confiscate the knives, then whatever the cult wanted to do couldn't be completed. After all, they looked for the knives, specific knives to commit the murders with. Take the knives away and you may not find out who committed the murders, but you sure would stop them from committing more. There couldn't be another set of knives kicking about, could there? These were special, special enough to be run through some nasty people for delivery. Hope decided that this pair would not leave with the knives, for she could stop more murders. Stop the cult in their tracks by getting hold of the knives.

Hope watched as Forbes dressed again, opening up his large bag and placing the monk's habit in it. Karen had returned to a more decent state, back in her jeans and jumper, the outfit she'd worn tucked away inside the bag. Hope watched as the knives were slowly put away, each lovingly handled. It was almost creepy as she saw Forbes take great delight through the torchlight.

Once the bag was packed, the pair took a few more moments embracing each other, whispering things to each other in the dark, and Hope tried to walk around to cut off their way back on the path. As she did so, she was aware that she couldn't see clearly beneath her, the ground full of twigs, loose branches, and small bushes. Ever so carefully Hope stepped on, afraid that one bad footstep could make a sound that would alert them to her presence.

Hope wasn't worried about dealing with them, even though there were two of them. She was tall, strong, and Forbes didn't look like he could even take a punch. Karen also seemed like she could be easily subdued. Circling around, Hope prepared to step out before them. As the couple swung the bag over Forbes's shoulder and proceeded along the path with the torch shining ahead, Hope stepped across their path, her jeans suddenly lit up by the torch light.

'Police! Stop right there. Forbes, put the bag down; put your hands behind your head.'

She watched the torchlight come up towards her face and she shielded her eyes from it.

'Put the torch down. Bag down now.'

Hope was surprised when the man did just that and the torch light shone along the little path lighting up her feet. In the dark, she could just about make him out, going down on his knees and putting his hands behind his head. Karen followed suit.

'Good,' said Hope. 'Good.' She reached behind her to take out a set of handcuffs. That was when she felt the thud and pitched forward onto the ground.

Somebody dropped onto her back, a knee driven between the shoulder blades causing her to cry out. She felt her hands being whipped behind her and her own cuffs were then snapped on her. The knee didn't leave her back until Forbes stood up, Karen standing with him.

A voice behind Hope said, 'What do you want us to do with her?'

'We should make a fine sacrifice for the master,' said Forbes.

71

He bent down looking into Hope's face. 'Yes, quite exquisite,' he said rubbing her cheek. 'You're in luck, for your boss I would gut right here, but the Master would like someone like you, sacrificed properly, defamed by the group first. No reason why we shouldn't have our fun as well.'

Hope tried to struggle, but again a knee was placed on her back and she was held tight. 'Drag her along and throw her in the boot of the car. We'll do it now.'

'Off to . . .'

'Yes,' said Forbes, before the man could complete the sentence. 'The ritual site.'

Hope felt the knee come off her back and she went to roll over, but her feet were grabbed by two sets of hands. She was dragged backward, the front of her body and her face bouncing over the path. Everything along her front was sore. She tried to lash out with her legs, managed to get one free and kick one of the men in the knees, but she was hit again in the back. It felt like some kind of nightstick or a truncheon. Whatever it was, it hurt. Again, she cried out.

'Shut her up,' said Forbes. Hope felt a gag being tied around her mouth. They continued to drag her, even when they reached the carpark, and she was dragged across the stones. She could feel the cuts on her chin. It was some time ago that Hope had been scarred with acid. She felt like the cuts going across her chin were as deep and blood must have been pouring from them.

As they reached the car, Hope was dragged up onto her feet. She saw the boot being opened. Forbes came up to her and the torchlight was passed up and down her.

'Oh yes,' he said, 'you will make a fine sacrifice.'

She couldn't make his face out from the edges of the

torchlight, but he looked wild, excited. Beside him, Karen smiled, clearly enjoying the position that Hope was in.

'Okay. Let's go. And don't worry,' he said to Hope, running a hand under her chin where some blood had gathered from the cuts made by being dragged across the stones. He tasted it and placed some on Karen's lips. Then he kissed her.

'You got too close, didn't you?' he said. 'Too close. You should have all kept out of it, but Macleod won't worry. His God will drive him on. What drives you on?'

Hope went to speak but the gag in her mouth stopped her, so Forbes pulled it down. 'The children yet to come,' said Hope, and spat in his face. He struck her with the back of his hand. Her chin hurt but Hope felt good. At least she was fighting back. Someone punched her hard in the stomach. She doubled over and she was knocked down to the ground. Two men picked her up, ready to throw her into the boot of the car.

Flashing blue lights were suddenly seen through the trees. A car screamed into the car park. The window was down. A megaphone blared. 'You're surrounded! Police! You're surrounded. Stand down! Stand down!'

Hope was dropped from about waist height, hit the ground hard, her chin contacting first and causing her teeth to crush together.

'Don't. Get her!'

Hope started to roll. All she could do was go over and over, trapping her hands between the ground and her back, and then freeing them as her front pressed to the ground. She rolled off into the undergrowth.

'Never mind. Just go. Go!'

The loudspeaker continued. 'You are surrounded. Police! On your knees!' From her position in some vegetation, Hope watched three cars pull away, but another one with blue lights flashing remained as the other cars disappeared from the car park. She heard footsteps coming towards her.

'Where are you? I can't see in this dark.' A pen torch came out.

Hope spoke into the darkness. 'Seoras, thank God, Seoras. I'm here, I'm here.' She heard the sounds of running feet. Then he knelt down beside her and pulled her close. 'What on earth are you doing?' he said. 'It's too dangerous. We do stuff together. You don't go off on your own.'

'I could have stopped them. They had the knives here. They had the knives.'

'But you didn't,' he said. 'But you didn't.' He had her sitting up now, pulling her close. 'Where were they going with you?' he asked.

Hope suddenly felt everything overtake her. 'Sacrifice site,' she said. 'They were going to sacrifice me. They were going to . . .' She thought about Forbes, his face, and his talk of the Master. She felt Macleod hold her tight as tears started to flow. 'Seoras, they would have . . .'

'I've got you,' he said. 'It's okay. I've got you.'

Chapter 10

The ambulance service checked Hope over after the incident in the woods and apart from some scrapes, she was deemed fit to continue. A small plaster was put onto her chin, as where the blood had flowed had not in truth been a particularly deep cut. Macleod had remained on scene until Jona Nakamura had turned up with her forensic team and set to work. Two of the main participants were known. Samuel Forbes and his would-be partner, Karen. Macleod immediately sent uniform round to Samuel Forbes's house where his wife advised he hadn't returned.

Macleod wondered if he would, now that he'd been compromised. Clearly, somebody knew who he was, had followed him, or at least that's how it might appear to him. Karen was certainly known. *How deep was their relationship? How high up the pecking order were they?* Everyone else that had messed up within the circle had been put to the sword. Macleod wondered would these two be next.

Did they carry enough rank? The scene they'd practiced out, did it specifically need to be them? Would that guarantee their safety until, well, he didn't want to think about what that scene entailed?

Macleod stood in his long coat, looking in at the wooded area where Jona had lit everything up like an UFO had just landed. He watched her team, sweeping over every bit of grass and tree stump, trying to dig out anything that could help. In a moment, he'd pick up Hope and head back to the office, just as soon as the paramedics had finished with her wounds.

When he'd briefly spoken to her earlier, she talked of the scene, how the couple had fornicated and intimated what they would do with the knives. He couldn't get his head around it. It was more than barbaric. Demonic. Is that what he was thinking? Once again, he was fighting to separate the job from his own faith. Part of him felt these people needed to be hunted down and stopped forever. While he'd gone out hunting them, he still saw the face of Gleary's niece. Although he hadn't seen what happened that night, it didn't stop his mind from imagining it.

'Still waiting here for me?'

Macleod turned and saw Hope smiling at him, but with a plaster stuck on her chin.

'Suits you, that one? Really does.'

'You never know. I might keep it as a fashion item. Anyway, you were clever.'

'Too many of them,' said Macleod. 'Way too many of them for me to handle. Looked like they were about to take you away as well. I'm not sure we would've got you back. No, I wouldn't have done it. I wouldn't have tried to stop . . .'

'Yes, you would. You would've tried to stop them.'

'We're desperate for this,' said Macleod, 'but the risks we're undertaking, it's too much. We need to be more careful. We said twos and we got caught out. Ross said to me, 'What harm could you come to, going to DIY stores?' There you go.'

'I'm okay, Seoras,' said Hope, 'I'm fine.'

'You nearly weren't. What if I didn't come up with that idea? What if I'd have strolled in here, tried to take them on with both of us heading off to some sort of ritual sacrifice?'

He felt a chill run through him. Normally, as an officer, he was immune to the murderer. Very rarely did their own lives ever become at risk. Sure, you had to work hard, and you might get emotionally and mentally damaged by the fact you hadn't prevented a murder, but you didn't think you were going to get murdered yourself. This case was too much. It wasn't right. He thought about his former detective, Kirsten Stewart, and thought maybe she was more appropriate to this line of investigation.

These people didn't mess about. Sometimes they shot first, even when the situation didn't demand it. Macleod shook his head. *No, this is what he was here for. This is what they were here for. They needed to get on with it.*

'I've called a meeting back at the office. Jona is going to stay and continue, see what she can come up with. I got a hold of Clarissa who has found a connection with the man in the photograph from the hotel and has found some fancy art person who seems to know a lot more about these rituals. I told Clarissa to bring her in.'

'Good,' said Hope. 'We could do with somebody on our side understanding what's going on. Maybe if we get ahead of their prep and their location, we can beat them to it.'

'Get to it before it starts,' said Macleod. 'I know. I feel it. Come on, you up to driving.'

'I got a scrape on the chin and my front's sore, but other than that, I'm okay, Seoras. I'm good to go.'

'Good,' said Macleod. 'Here's the keys. I'll get a constable to

77

drive yours up. I've done enough driving for one night.'

The pair drove in silence, listening to a late-night radio station until they arrived back at Inverness Police Station. When Macleod walked through the door, he heard Ross stand up and simply nodded towards him before entering his own office. The lights were switched on, and Hope marched through to sit down at the little round table. She heard Ross come in behind her a few minutes later, coffee in cups.

'Where's Clarissa with her newbie?' asked Macleod.

'I've just buzzed her. She was down in the canteen. Apparently, the woman was hungry,' said Ross.

'Ross, tell her to get up here. Let's get on with it.'

Ross disappeared and Macleod sat down with his coffee in front of him. Hope pulled out a notebook and began writing in it.

'What are you doing?' asked Macleod.

'I'm remembering what they did and how they did it.'

Macleod looked over. 'That looks like some badly drawn karma sutra.'

Hope raised her eyes. 'That's what it felt like,' she said.

The office door was knocked and then Clarissa barged on through, waving at a woman behind her to enter. Macleod looked up and a young woman of maybe twenty-five with long, black boots, tight, leather trousers, and a grey jacket stood in the doorway. The jacket was swept off, dumped in one of the chairs and the woman sat down, looking across at Macleod. She had a thin strap top on, and Macleod thought she could be going out for a romantic dinner and when she smiled, the teeth looked like the outside of a new kitchen appliance, perfectly white.

'May I present to everyone, Abby Scarlet. Abby's an expert

on what these people are trying to do.'

'Not from personal practice,' said Abby quickly.

'I've had dealings with Abby in the past,' said Clarissa. 'She is an expert in her field. I suggest we take what she has to say very seriously. Abby, this is Detective Inspector Seoras Macleod who you've probably seen on the telly. However, the rest of us here are the engine room of the team. Ross, who we've talked about, and this is Detective Sergeant Hope McGrath who appears to have a rather pale plaster on her chin.'

'Thanks for pointing that out', said Hope. 'I was the one who saw what happened down in the forest.'

'Really?' said Abby, 'and did they act it out?'

'They did,' said Hope. 'It was quite grotesque. Highly sexualised, yet quite grotesque.'

'It sounds about right,' said Abby. 'Tell me about it.'

Hope pushed over the pad in front of her. 'That's what I've been trying to do. Write it down. Just formalise it before I forget it.'

'This looks like some early version of the Karma Sutra.' Hope flashed her eyes over at Macleod who simply nodded.

'It'd be better if you actually told me straight, though,' said Abby, 'I can ask you questions in between if needs be.'

Hope relayed all that she'd seen including the graphic details. Abby sat simply nodding, occasionally asking to clarify the exact position the couple had been in or where they had swung a knife. Ross sat open-mouthed, rather bemused at the whole thing.

'Can you help us?' asked Macleod once Hope had finished speaking.

'I can, Inspector, and I most definitely will. I fear you could be in a lot of trouble.'

'We've already had several kids and adults die,' said Ross. 'Could you clarify what you mean by a lot of trouble?'

'The thing is,' said Abby, 'I've spoken to Clarissa already about a certain book that describes what your sergeant saw tonight.' Abby pulled out the plastic folder and started dishing out pages of symbols which nobody in the team recognised. 'I've decoded this or rather translated it. It is an actual language albeit demonic.'

Macleod held up a hand. 'Hold on a minute here,' he said. 'What do you mean the language is demonic?'

'I mean it's the language of demons. You don't have to believe it is the language of demons. It's a language that is associated with demons that apparently humans translate or can understand, and it can be translated into English.'

'You're not going to tell me that there's actual demons involved,' said Macleod. 'It's very easy to get confused when we talk about murders such as this.'

'I'll be straight with you, Inspector,' said Abby. She stood up, spinning behind her chair and then leaning forward, taking the attention of the entire table. 'What has been done tonight is a practice for a ritual in which seven children will die. There are usually approximately nine people who will carry it out, seven sitting, holding the children, and two others, one acting like a sacrifice, the other carrying out the killings. The man tonight would be doing that. The woman dressed as she was and parading as she did, was enacting a ritual to bring up a pestilence on the world encouraging the arrival of their master.'

'Their master being?' asked Ross.

'The devil. Satan. This is Satanism. Call it what you will. This is a definite form of Satanism.'

Macleod choked. He felt it. 'Are you saying that this thing will work?' asked Macleod.

'Inspector, I'm not going to sit here and tell you what will happen is some demon will appear, run around, and start taking over the earth. All I'm doing is following what the book says and what these people are doing. Understand me that what happens when this occurs, I don't know. It will involve seven children dying. The book says that there's a preparation. Five go before and then there's this mass ritual at the end. The way is laid and then the act is done. Five before seven at once.'

'Dear God,' said Ross. 'Seven? They kill seven of them at once?'

'Yes,' said Abby. 'I don't know if this has ever been enacted. The knives, however, are the knives of Gog.'

'The knives of Gog?' queried Hope.

'Revelation,' said Macleod, 'Magog and Gog, end of the world. Never heard of those knives though.'

'I already talked to Clarissa about this,' said Abby. 'Comes out of the dark ages. Are they for real? Who knows? What I do know is that somebody wanted them bad enough that they came to me and asked about getting them. I did not assist with that partly because I know what it entails. I have a fascination with this sort of stuff. Trust me, Inspector, I do, but never do I ever want to see anyone harmed from it. Certainly, not killed from it. You can take that from me.' Macleod glanced over at Clarissa who gave a simple nod.

'You might find Abby a bit weird,' said Clarissa. 'Trust me; she's been a pain in my backside often enough when I was working arts, but she knows what she's on about and she's not that sort of person. She wouldn't harm children. In fact, generally, she wouldn't harm people. She'd just rob them blind.'

81

'That's very touching of you,' said Abby.

'Hang on,' said Macleod. 'Hang on. So, this is a ritual?'

'Yes.'

'Tell me more about it.'

'Well, the idea is that you kill five kids beforehand and then you kill seven at once and you use the knives of Gog to do it,' said Abby.

'What about the children? Any child? Anyone? Can we narrow this down?' said Macleod.

'Orphans or those of single mothers. It's from the Bible, the line where they say true Christianity is looking after the orphan and the widow.'

'Those that cannot look after themselves,' said Macleod. 'Yes, but it was beholden to the Christians in that community to look after them because they couldn't support themselves. There was no welfare system. There was nothing. Once you were a widow, that was it. If your husband's brother or someone else didn't look after you, you were stuffed.'

'Exactly. Well, this is taking the very people you're meant to care for,' said Abby.

'And killing them,' said Macleod, 'killing them as affront to God. A blessing to the devil.'

'You've got it. You've got it in one.'

'If someone's prepared to do this, and not just that,' said Macleod, 'but if someone's prepared to practice it, go to this length, go to the point of killing of other people when we get close then we may have . . .'

'True believers,' said Abby. 'People that actually believe this actually believe if they do this, they're going to see their master rise.'

'Therefore, if they're deluded or not, it doesn't actually

matter, does it?' said Macleod.

'We know two of them,' said Hope. 'We saw two of them there tonight with the man with a broken nose. That's the one you saw, Abby, wasn't it?'

'Yes,' she said.

'Well, who do we know beyond that?' asked Ross. 'We haven't got anybody beyond that, have we? And there's going to be nine participants in the ritual. That's three we know; we have to find them. One, we've got a partial ID on but need to know the name of and find, and six others we've got to find. We don't know how quick it's going to happen, how long we have to stop this killing of seven kids.'

'We'll need to find a ritual site,' said Hope. 'We need to find out where it's going to happen. Abby, we need to know of anything significant in the location so we can get there first.'

'More than that,' said Macleod. 'Five, prepare the way. Seven at the end. We haven't had number five yet. There's another one coming first. We need to find out where.'

Chapter 11

Ross stood in front of the whiteboard in Macleod's office with twelve spaces for names. Before him, at the round table, sat Macleod, Hope, Clarissa, and Abby. The faces were tired. On the table, there were several cups of coffee amidst drawings that helped Abby's explanation of how she had come to understand the ritual.

Macleod had been quite impressed with her. She was very open about what she'd obtained illegally, after giving a disclaimer to say that whatever she said would be denied by her if it came to the court of law. Macleod didn't blame her, and in truth, what she'd done had not been good. She was a thief, but she was also an intelligent woman, one who was heavily involved in that occult world, in the artefacts and images. But he noted it was with horrified interest, as opposed to a practised individual.

'We've got twelve people in the circle originally,' said Ross, 'because we have twelve knives of Gog, four of which have been used. Who do we know that's on the list? Samuel Forbes, now on the run. Karen Whitelaw on the run with Samuel Forbes. Broken-nose-man seems to turn up everywhere, almost like an enforcer of the group. Winston Arnold called to finish off some of the group, instructions received from his bookshop. He may not know that we are onto him. So far, all investigations into him have been done quietly.'

'What about the dead?' asked Macleod.

'The Mackie brothers,' continued Ross, 'both definitely in the group. Nathan had carried out one killing, sleeping with his sister in the process. Kyle carried out Nathan's murder, as far as we understand it. Kyle also went to carry out the killing of Daniel, the child I'm hoping to adopt. Kyle was also finished off by the group, possibly because of bringing in a child closely linked to one of us.'

Macleod felt lost at this point and stared for longer than normal, almost uneasy with what had just been spoken about.

'As I see it,' continued Ross, 'Samuel Forbes and Karen Whitelaw have both gone to ground and are going to be hard to find. We can talk to Samuel Forbes's wife, we can go to the DIY store and find out more about Karen, but if they've gone to ground, they've gone to hide. As for Broken-nose-man, we are still waiting for anything to come back via Abby. Winston Arnold, however, as far as we understand, doesn't know we're onto him. That's probably the best place to go.'

'Indeed,' said Macleod, 'good place to start. He's all the way down in the borders and as far as they know it, we haven't been there. There's been no police presence, just me and Clarissa there when we shouldn't have been. I think you're right, Ross. We need to get down there and investigate. Clarissa, you go. You've been before.'

'Should I accompany?' asked Ross.

'No, you stay here, get onto the photofit with the Broken-nose man, get onto photographs of Samuel Forbes, Karen Whitelaw, getting them out there, but not of Winston Arnold.

Let's keep him under wraps. His name doesn't go out of here. Anyone involved in the investigation will know about him already, but don't push it any further.'

Macleod watched the nods around the team, but Clarissa looked concerned. 'I might have to go on my own then?' she asked.

'No, take a constable with you. Don't go down with a full squad but contact the local police quietly. Let them know, or at least let somebody at the top know what you're doing, so that if you have to call in for backup, it comes quick. We don't know who's involved in this,' said Macleod.

'One thing that worries me,' he continued, 'is that with twelve people in such a group which has been kept so well under wraps, they may have people involved with them who can get into our lines of inquiry, who might understand what we do, how we do it, and actually be there advising them to get out quick. The case is obviously a big one. The press is all over it. At the moment, they're in our favour, but that can change quickly as well. The last thing we need to do is let them know we're coming.'

'True,' said Hope, 'this group doesn't hang about with people.'

'We got fortunate so far,' agreed Macleod. 'Me, Clarissa, Hope, even Ross has had a shady couple of dealings. Miss Scarlet, keep everything under wraps. Do not reach out anywhere, unless asked to by us. If you're needing to go to the art world, run it through Clarissa. She understands that world and she'll understand the side of it that you won't, namely, who's liable to rat on us. She's a good judge of character.'

'How are we going to do the search for Forbes and Whitelaw?' asked Ross.

'I'll get onto that with Hope,' said Macleod. 'We'll do the

footwork while you get through the computer records. Spread out. I want this manhunt organised well, Ross. I want you on top of it and don't want you dragged off elsewhere. This could be the key, but also, liaise with Jona, see if she's dug anything up from tonight.

'Miss Scarlet, you've told us so much about that I want you to go back over the previous incidents in the previous murders. I want you to look at the symbols. I want you to tell me if there's anything else that I should know. Other than that, let's get on it.'

'Can I ask when you guys sleep?' asked Abby. 'It's just Clarissa came last night, we've been up all night, and now we're off doing this again. Is that normal?'

Ross shook his head. 'No, we're usually up a lot longer than this.'

'If you can just stay for a moment,' said Macleod to Abby. The rest of the team stood up, and filed out into the other office, and Macleod closed the door after them.

'I'm very appreciative of you coming in and helping out like this. Don't get me wrong, I don't approve of what you do and the way you operate, and I'm sure Clarissa doesn't either, but she made a wise decision bringing you in.'

'Well, this is kids. This is gross murder,' said Abby. 'That's not what I'm about.'

'I get that,' said Macleod, 'I really do.'

'But what about you, Inspector? You clearly know your Bible. You're not just another officer approaching something. The way you think, the way you see it, this is more than an investigation to you, isn't it?'

'As it is to you,' said Macleod. 'The last thing you need is for people to go around believing in this. It's all very fascinating and interesting, until they decide to act it out. Now you're wondering have you encouraged it? Have you introduced anyone to this in the past?'

'It did cross my mind,' said Abby, 'but you're looking at this not just from the point of view of killing off innocent children, are you? What if this really does cause a curse in the land, if it does let him roam free? It's going through your mind, isn't it, Inspector?'

'Of course, it is. You can't believe the things I believe without wondering if this is part of it, but ultimately, it's irrelevant. We stop them killing the children, that's the important bit. We stop them doing that, nothing else gets put to the test, whether it'll happen or not.'

'One of the things I didn't talk about,' said Abby, 'is that in the paperwork in the tale, it talks about what to do to bring about the master's rise. It also warns about those coming to prevent it.'

'You're not going to tell me it's foretold of an old man in a raincoat with a nice tie charging to the rescue?'

Abbey laughed. 'No,' she said, 'but it does talk about the group of people. It does talk about the believer. It might just be a metaphor. It might just be a generalisation to be aware of the believer.'

'The only thing I believe at the moment is that we're facing a lot of true believers. They'll do anything to bring about his will. You help me get that sorted. You help me prevent that, and I'll be a happy man.'

'Whatever you need, Inspector,' she said. She turned away, but Macleod called to her. 'Can you tell me, was Clarissa happy coming to you?'

'She's never been happy. I'm the case that she couldn't solve.

Oh, she knew I did it, but she couldn't prove it.'

'She must think a lot of you,' said Macleod. 'She really must.'

'Your Constable Ross is quite something, isn't he?'

'Very much,' said Macleod. 'He's deeply tied into the case though as well. They attempted to kill the child he was looking to adopt.'

'He said something about that. I take it his spouse must have been annoyed at that too. Must be rough on them.'

'Very much so, but they're getting through it. They may even still adopt. He seems to have recovered.'

'Ross does look good.'

'I wasn't speaking about Ross. I meant his spouse. Angus seems to have recovered as well.'

Macleod saw Abby's face fall.

'I might have known,' she said.' The woman walked out quickly from the office, leaving Macleod a little bemused with how she was suddenly so interested, and then just dropped the matter. As the door went to close, Macleod saw it being opened again. DCI Lawson entered, dressed in jeans and a jumper.

'Detective Chief Inspector,' said Macleod.

'It's just Alan.'

'Alan. I prefer DCI Lawson.'

'No, Seoras. It's just Alan. I'm kind of being detached at the moment, being kept away. Assistant Chief Constable's had a word. I'll be moving on, heading elsewhere. Just got a few things to pick up.'

'Is there anything I can help you with?' asked Macleod. 'I am actually quite busy.'

'Well, I just wanted to drop in and say, sorry. I kind of screwed it up, didn't I?'

'You hung me out to dry,' said Macleod. 'Around me here is a team. Sometimes they get it wrong, sometimes I get it wrong, but we're a team. We call each other together to make sure we get it right, more often than not. You seemed to miss that.'

'I guess I did. That Sergeant McGrath's something else,' said Lawson. 'She backed you all the way. Backed you all the way, even though to do so meant she wouldn't get to be out forward to be a DI.'

'That's why she'll be a DI one day and the best. Hope doesn't suffer fools,' said Macleod.

'That's what I've been, is it? I've been a fool. Well, I guess you're right,' said Lawson. 'I guess so. Are you getting anywhere with the case?'

'Well, trying to work out whom we know amongst them. We know Winston Arnold.'

'Yes, he was part of the pool of suspects when I was in, but it was coming from someone else. Hope said it was her source and never told me who her source was, but you did well, Seoras. You did well. It's not easy operating on the outside.'

'I guess not,' said Macleod. 'If she ever tells me who that source is, I will go and shake them by the hand. They've got me back in the job.'

'Indeed,' said Lawson. He stepped forward and put out his hand. 'Look, no hard feelings. I'm far from the best copper, but I am an honest one.'

The door flew open behind. 'That's me off to Winston Arnold,' said Clarissa. Then she clocked that Lawson was in the room. 'Oh, I'm sorry,' said Clarissa. 'I didn't realise. I hope you've apologised to him.'

'It's okay, Clarissa,' said Macleod. 'Alan's leaving. He did indeed just come in to apologise. He'll be on his way very shortly.'

'All the best,' Lawson said to Macleod. 'To all of you. I genuinely mean that.'

'And to you, Alan. Hope the next stage of your life works out better for you.'

'Indeed, Seoras. Indeed.' Macleod watched the man turn and walk out of the office.

'He has a damn cheek,' said Clarissa. 'Should have punched him one.'

'Get to Winston Arnold.'

'But I'm right though, aren't I? You should have . . .'

'Get to Winston Arnold,' said Macleod.

'All right. Being up all night got you like this?'

'Go. Just go.'

Chapter 12

The little green sports car arrived in the borders after a busy drive down. The traffic had been reasonable considering it was winter, and Clarissa had stopped twice for coffee as she felt tired on the journey. Constable Rippon was sitting beside her, but at no point did Clarissa think about handing over the keys. She didn't give the little green sports car to anyone, not unless she really had to.

The border town was suffering from a cold and gloomy day, and the light drizzle made everybody even colder. Clarissa parked up a little distance from Winston Arnold's shop and saw the butcher she'd spoken with previously. Part of her thought about picking up a steak for tonight, maybe even bringing back four or five for the team. They didn't eat well when things got like this, possibly because you felt tired. You got into the habit of skipping food, so you needed to break that, needed to make sure everyone was feeling on form, or at least as much as much as you could, given the circumstances.

Constable Rippon was dressed in casual jeans and a jumper and looked like a younger niece of Clarissa's. Truth was Clarissa was getting fed up with being surrounded by younger women. At least with Ross, it didn't look so bad. She kept reminding herself that some men preferred a little bit more experience, and maturity on the head of their woman. *How did she ever get to this age still needing a man in her life?*

She knew there were plenty of women who didn't. Women who just seemed to be quite happy at this age to be on their own or with whatever animal, or even platonic friend, but not Clarissa. There was too much fire still inside her. At least that's what she liked to say. Maybe she was just lonely. Maybe she just didn't do a fireside rug. Well, better to have somebody cuddle up to you. Whatever, it wasn't going to get the job done here today, so she stepped out of the car, shawl around her, out into the rain, and made for the butcher's.

'It's you again. I haven't seen you about.'

'No, no. Actually, I'm just coming to ask you, do you know if Winston Arnold is in, has he come back at all?'

'He's in there at the moment,' said the butcher. 'Saw him go in about, oh, two or three minutes ago. Hasn't been back in ages either. Just returning back to the store. I said hello to him and he said he'd been up Inverness way, whatever he'd been at.'

'Well, thank you,' said Clarissa, and turned on her heel.

'Is that it? You want to buy some meat with that?'

'I'll be back for some in a bit,' she said, then tried to work at how she was going to do that with someone in handcuffs. She stepped out of the butcher's, waved over at Constable Rippon, and together the pair of them approached Winston Arnold's bookshop. Clarissa tried the door, and as she looked inside saw Arnold in the recesses. There was a bell which rang as the door opened, and Clarissa shouted in. 'Hello, just looking to top up some books while we're on holiday. Don't know if you'd have my sort of thing.'

'You're welcome to come in,' said the man, but he sounded rather distracted. Clarissa walked into the shop, Rippon following her, and she saw Winston Arnold looking at a letter. He began to cry, sobbing, and then he looked around, 'Can I help you?' he asked.

'I need you to come with me. I'm Detective Sergeant Clarissa Urquhart, and we need to take you in for questioning. This is Constable Rippon, who's going to put some handcuffs on you. If you'd like to come quietly, I'm sure we can avoid a fuss.'

Winston Arnold put his hands out, tears still streaming down his face, the letter now abandoned on the table in front of him. Clarissa picked up her phone and called Macleod.

'We got him, Seoras, Winston Arnold. He's been in here about five minutes, first time back in a while and we've got him. I'll stick him in the car and bring him back up.'

'Get him in a police car and bring him up,' said Macleod. 'No risks. Now you've got him just in case anyone's watching. In fact, ring your backup. Make sure you've got cover all the way out there until you get him up to here.'

'You sound very on edge with this, Seoras,' said Clarissa. 'We've got him. He's coming quietly.'

'Backup,' said Macleod. 'Keep your wits about you until you're up here.'

Clarissa shook her head but closed down the call. 'Boss says bring him up. I'm just going to call for the backup first.'

'But we've got him?' said Rippon.

'I know. It's just the boss; we do as he says.'

Clarissa picked up the phone again dialling the local station and asking for a few more constables to join her. They advised there'd be another car on the way. After nodding approvingly, Clarissa put her phone away and turned to Winston Arnold.

The man was still crying.

'You shouldn't really have come back, should you?' said Clarissa, 'but you're going to tell us everything.'

Once again, the man cried, and then he sat down on the floor.

'Don't mess me about,' said Clarissa. 'Constable, take him.' She tried to lift him up, but the man laughed.

'I'm not going anywhere. This is where I'm staying. This is where I will go home. This is me.'

'That's not how it works,' said Clarissa. 'If we have to manhandle you, we will do, get you into the car.'

'I could try now, Sergeant.'

'Don't, Rippon. It's okay. We've got two more coming. Do this as a team; it'll be a lot easier.'

Clarissa stood with her back to one of the bookshelves, and then looked out towards the front window. The day wasn't getting any better. The rain had continued but was now much stronger. If only the guy would just get up and get in the car, they could get underway, nice and dry. While she waited, Clarissa took a walk along the bookshelves, happy that Rippon had an eye on the man, and he wasn't going anywhere. She pulled out one book with heavy occult symbols in the front.

Opening it, she saw beasts with human heads, beast heads with a human body, all mixed up, intertwined and at times seemingly copulating together in a fashion that she found utterly repulsive.

'Who buys rubbish like this?' she said. 'You seriously sell this?'

Winston Arnold sniffed back some tears and looked up at her. 'That's a quality book,' he said, 'but you wouldn't understand it. You don't understand any of it, do you? Can't you see what

95

we're doing?

Clarissa wanted to tell him that they understood an awful lot. They'd seen the ritual they were going to perform. They knew all about it, all about the knives and now one of those who had to partake in it would be in custody. Could they still do it? Could they get a replacement? Did Winston Arnold actually have a knife located somewhere? If so, it couldn't happen. After all, the knives of Gog were at the centre of this, weren't they?

Clarissa shook her head. *Who fell for this sort of baloney? Who would actually believe this? Maybe it was all a game. Maybe it was just a bit of fun they indulged that had got out of hand. Out of hand when you kill a kid and put symbols on them. Too much,* she thought. *Way, way too much.*

Clarissa put the book back, pulled out several more, each having such weird pictures within them. The collection was at the rear of the shop. Maybe there were worse upstairs. Clarissa remembered being in here with Macleod, avoiding that main window but now she strode to it and looked out wondering when the backup was coming. She turned on her heel and looked back at the man. He seemed to have stopped his tears from flowing. Instead, he was looking at her, almost with a grin.

'What do you think you are smiling at?' asked Clarissa. 'Game's up. The game is up. You murdered kids. You'll get done for that. You'll get years. Public will demand it, never mind what they do. Also, wherever you go, you killed kids, you harmed kids. A large part of the criminal community don't like people like you so you'll get what you deserve even if it's not from a judge. If you tell us who the rest of them are, you never know, they might put you in solitary. You might be the person that they let off. Well, not let off, but at least you'll have a life. You'll not be afraid that someone's going to come and give you a kicking every day. They'll do more than that. They'll happily break ribs. Maybe they'll do a lot more than that. Do you understand?'

He looked up at her and started laughing. 'What's up with you?' asked Clarissa. 'What have you got to laugh about?'

The laugh continued, almost hysterical. Then the man started to sing, only the language was nothing that Clarissa understood. She'd heard many European languages, many foreign ones as well. Asian languages, some of which were quite beautiful. A lot of them she couldn't speak, but she'd known them. Even the Middle East. But this was different. She knew she recognised the phrasing, for Abby had said the same type of thing when she was reading that manuscript.

Clarissa glowered at the man. 'You can cut that out.' He murmured more phrases and then one over and over again, over and over again. 'What does that mean?' asked Clarissa. 'What are you saying?'

'Beelzebub, take me now?' said the man laughing. Clarissa watched the man's eyes as they shot across the shop. She saw the brown package. It was small, but it was no distance from the man, maybe three metres. Then the man started chanting again the same thing over and over again asking for his master to take him.

'Rippon out. Out now.'

'What do you mean?'

Clarissa grabbed her and hobbled her way to the door as quick as she could. She grabbed it, throwing it open, Rippon in her grasp, half stumbling, unsure what was happening.

With the door open, Clarissa heard the blast from behind

then felt the force of it throwing her out onto the street. Together with Rippon, she crashed hard down onto the pavement rolling and deafened by the explosion and then the shattering of glass all around her.

The front window had blown out of the shop, and only for the fact that her shawl had blown up and over the top of her face had she been stopped from having glass cutting into her skin. As she tried to get up, she felt glass cutting her hands. Looking over, Clarissa saw Rippon's face amess with blood. The glass had gone into the side of her face, but the woman was still moving.

'Easy,' said Clarissa. 'Can you get up? Don't use your hands. Don't use your hands on the ground. Use your elbows or something. Use your elbows.'

'What's happened?' Another voice through her ringing ears. She barely recognised the butcher from next door who had come out of his shop. The blast had been strong knocking her off her feet. It had taken out the windows, but the wall through to the butcher shop next door was still intact.

Maybe it'd been damaged structurally, who would know? A siren began to fill the air. Clarissa stumbled over towards the shop entrance. There was dust in the air, and she coughed back a mouthful of it before she looked around again, somewhat unsteady on her feet. Rippon was up on her knees now, but the blood was still running down the side of her face and the butcher had run over to her placing his apron across her face, trying to pat down some of the blood.

'Get an ambulance,' shouted Clarissa. 'Somebody, get an ambulance.'

She looked inside the shop again. There was paper everywhere and then she saw him, or at least part of him. As she scanned the shop she realised that Winston Arnold wouldn't be coming back up to the office. He had known. He had known they were going to blow the place to kingdom come. Had it been in that letter? All he had done was worship his blasted devil. What sort of a man was this that happily accepted a bomb? He could have run, he could have got out, he could have told them, but instead, he was waiting to take them with him.

Clarissa shook her head. Her ears were still ringing. She could hear people, though not clearly. She'd heard the butcher, but not that well.

He'd known something, she suddenly thought. *Seoras had said, 'Be careful.' Seoras said. What the heck had Seoras known? What had he thought?*

An arm went around Clarissa and she saw a man in a large green jacket. 'It's okay, love. It's okay. Was there anyone else in there?'

'One,' said Clarissa slowly, 'but he's not coming back out.'

Chapter 13

Macleod marched into the office, pushed open his own private door through to his workspace, and slammed it behind him. Walking over to the desk, he picked up a pen, gripping it, and then bounced it hard off the top of the desk. He watched as it hit the chair, and then fell down to the ground. It was a cheap plastic barrel, but he felt some dismay as he saw it broken in two halves on the floor. He took a deep breath, walked slowly around the back of the chair, picked up the pen, and dropped it into the wastepaper bin. *I could have lost her*, he thought. *Could have lost Clarissa. What sort of people blow themselves up, or allow themselves to be blown up?*

The explosion in the small border's town was all over the press, and they were asking the question whether this was a terrorist attack. Macleod had got hold of the correct people quickly, advising that it wasn't. He'd also made sure that Clarissa was away from the scene as fast as she could be. The border police could, by all means, question her, but in private; the last thing he needed was her face being put on a public camera and a link being made to these murders. Although she was one of the less recognisable figures of Macleod's team, which surprised Macleod given how she dressed, she would soon get tagged to him.

There was a rap at the door behind him.

'You okay, Seoras. You know she's fine.'

'Of course, I know she's fine. It's just everything. She's not used to dealing with this, Hope. This is not what we signed up for.'

'We always know there are risks.'

'We nearly lost her twice now.'

'You told me she was a tough old bird, streetwise.'

'She is,' said Macleod. 'That's why they got out. That's why Rippon's alive as well. Clarissa clocked it. That's what she told me on the phone, she clocked it. Got them to run, and made sure Rippon followed her. They only just got out the door when the bomb went off. Fortunately, it wasn't a big one. Big enough to reach Winston Arnold, but not big enough to take Clarissa out as well, not when she'd put some distance between them.'

'But she's basically fine,' said Hope. 'I mean cuts and bruises, but that's it.'

'I know,' he said, 'and she's screaming to get back into this. 'Can't let the children down.' She said that to me. 'Can't let the children down.' It's getting too emotional, and we're running out of places to go with this investigation. Samuel Forbes and Karen Whitelaw are nowhere to be seen, gone to ground. I take it you haven't found anything more on them.'

'No,' said Hope, 'it's like they've gone off the face of the earth. They're probably hiding out in one of the other members' houses. We'll never find them if we don't know who that member is. Can't search every house in Inverness.'

Macleod didn't turn around, but instead stared out of the

window as he was so prone to do, hoping the brain would engage and come up with something different.

'How would you perform the ritual?' he said suddenly.

'Come again.'

'Hope,' said Macleod, turning around, 'how would you perform the ritual? Where would your items come from? Have to order some of this stuff, these gowns. There must be things to do with a ceremony. You have to order the knives, obviously, but they're special. They're different. What about the other things? You also have to clean up, don't you, can't leave traces behind. Tell Ross to get onto that. See if we can find any gowns being ordered, manufactured, or where you would buy them. Are they coming off websites? If so, let's trawl for who's bought them.'

'He's probably thought of that already, Seoras, but I'll mention it to him. Are you all right?'

'Define all right.'

'That's not you,' said Hope.

'It's hit me this one. It's hit me. When we were stuck in the basement together, the water coming up, well, she kind of said a few things.'

'Oh, I know she's keen on you,' said Hope.

'Yes. Well, as much as I'm not keen on her and I have no intentions of any romantic interest in that way,' Macleod said quietly, 'she kind of gets to you, doesn't she? She gets under your skin as a person. They know Clarissa the Rottweiler, the angry one, the one who's going to come in and boot people, shake them up.'

'And Seoras is the cold inspector, and they don't know you either. They don't know the care that you put into the cases, into people, looking out for them, into your colleagues.'

'Nearly lost her, Hope. Nearly lost her.'

She put her hand upon his shoulder, steadying him, and he thought for a moment, he might even shed a few tears. But he took a quick sniff and gave a nod, indicating that Hope should drop the arm.

His phone rang, and Macleod picked it up from the desk, holding his hand up, indicating that Hope should remain quiet.

'Jona,' he said, 'what have we got down there?'

'Been all over it, Seoras, up, down, here, and there. So many twigs, leaves, we can't get clear casts of feet. In fact, the clearest we've got was Hope's. There's the odd partial one, but it's not matching up to anything we find elsewhere. I'm afraid it's looking like a bust from this end. We may pick up the odd hair fragment or similar, but it's going to be Samuel or Karen, or their accomplices. Well, we've grabbed DNA from the other places, and we'll hold it on file, but until we find the people, we don't have the requisite DNA to match it against.'

'Okay, Jona, are you liaising with the team on the bomb site and the borders?'

'Of course, Seoras. Very standard bomb. Said it wouldn't have taken an awful lot to make up. They're going to try and trace it though, see what they can tag to local distributors, see where any of the elements came from, get addresses, do the usual thing, but it's not easy, especially with bombs. The core thing you want to look at has been blown to pieces. I hear they're searching through the bookstore as well, see if they can find any more of those messages, but nothing so far.'

'Well, keep on it, Jona. Even if we don't find the lead this way, when it all comes out in the wash, DNA will prove where people were. Keep going.'

'It's okay, Seoras. Of course, I'll keep going. Do you think that Clarissa is okay?'

'Tough old bird,' he said, 'but yes, Jona, she's fine.'

He put the phone down, and Hope looked over at him. 'Jona's not come up with anything either,' he said. 'Do you know something? It's funny being back in. It's funny being back in and having to go down all these routes that we normally go.'

'Thought you'd have been used to this. This is your bread and butter. Didn't think you'd be too happy working on the outside.'

'I wasn't, especially contacting Gleary, but it moved things on. It moved it forward. We got where we needed to be. When we're going down this route, the standard route, what we should do, how we should operate, they're ahead of us. They're not leaving anything behind. There's nothing to grab hold of. We're left waiting on a hit from a photograph over someone's shoulder, and no doubt when we find that person, they'll have killed them or blown them to pieces.' He turned and kicked the table.

'You be careful with that,' said Hope. 'It's a bit stronger than the pen.'

'We need to push this,' he said. 'We need to push this.'

'In what way?'

'Someone knew Clarissa was coming. Someone must have watched for her. Why would you plant the bomb with Winston Arnold? Why?'

'To take him out,' said Hope.

'He came back to his place of work. He came back to his normal address. Just wait inside, cut his throat. Do it simply. Why look to blow up other people? Just kill him. The point was to silence the person. I'm beginning to feel that Winston Arnold knew what was coming, accepted his fate, didn't run for it, because they weren't just after Winston Arnold.'

'You think they laid a trap for Clarissa?'

'They laid a trap for me and her before. Settling a score, Hope, or more bloodshed. Maybe they see that as worship. Maybe they see that as offering more, especially, when they've messed up some of the other stuff.'

'They didn't mess up, did they though? We found them. We got there. We saved Daniel.'

'And this was payback,' said Macleod.

'But how did they know Clarissa was going to be there?' asked Hope.

'Exactly,' said Macleod.

'Do we have a mole on the team? Do you think somebody in here is actually working for them?'

'Who knew Clarissa was going?' asked Macleod suddenly. 'You did, I did. Abby? She was about.'

'And Ross,' said Hope. 'The four of us aren't going to do anything. Maybe Abby should be looked into. Maybe.'

'No,' said Macleod. 'No, Clarissa vouched for her. Clarissa had every reason not to like her, not to bring her in, not to trust her, but she did, but she doesn't do that lightly. She's the last person to let somebody come in if she's got any doubt about them. The last person to not give a warning about them.'

'Well, that's us then. That's the five of us. Unless Rippon managed to blurt one out.'

'Rippon didn't get told where she was going until they left,' said Macleod. 'We wanted to keep everything quiet. Clarissa might have told some people down on the borders force, but again, on the quiet. It's a possible leak, but . . .' And then Macleod raised his fist, squeezing it.

'What?' asked Hope.

'He came in here. Blast it, he came in here.'

'Who?'

'Lawson. DCI Lawson. He came in that morning. I'm packing up, I'm doing this. Came in to apologise. He's not an apologising man. Clarissa walked in, blurted it out then. I didn't think anything of it, because he knew about Winston Arnold anyway. If they had thought of Winston Arnold as a problem, they'd have killed him before that. He knew we were onto him, knew he'd been there, or at least had occasioned a visit.'

'Are you sure about that though?' said Hope. 'I mean, I know he was a buffoon, I know he was an idiot, I know he was . . .'

'You know what?'

'When he tried to get me on board with him,' said Hope, 'he pandered to how I looked, quite the old fart with it. Told me how good-looking I was. Even when I told him no and told him I was standing up for you, he just wanted it all to go away, nice and quiet.'

'He took me off the case,' said Macleod. 'Took me off the case. Split the team.'

Macleod picked up the phone, dialled a number, and then sat back in his chair holding the phone to his ear, a smile on his lips.

'Hello, Chief Inspector,' said Macleod. 'I'm just wondering if you could come in. I need to discuss something with you. Something from the case when I was off. It's just that Chief Constable's asking about it. Over the phone? No, I'm sorry. I can't do. You'll need to come in. It's nothing deeply important. Really tying things up just to make sure I haven't missed anything. It's not easy working from afar. I was out of the loop, and you were in it. Just need to make sure that some paperwork is sorted out. Okay, I'll come to you. I can do that. Taking some time out? You're the lucky one,' said Macleod. 'We'll do this beforehand though. Appreciate it. Thank you, Alan. I'll see you shortly.'

Macleod put the phone down and saw Hope looking at him.

'What?' he said. 'What's the matter?'

'Nothing's the matter. You call her the Rottweiler, and you're just a cold one. You're not cold at the moment. Fires are burning now.'

'We nearly lost her, Hope. We nearly lost her. Somebody tried to blow my sergeant to kingdom come. I just don't know if I'd be able to keep my arms off him when we get there.'

Macleod looked down and saw his hand, fists clenched, knuckles white.

'Well, just make sure Ross doesn't get in before you. He's like a kettle overboiling in there, and make sure you don't explode. We need leads, Seoras. We need leads, not revenge.'

'And leads we'll get,' said the Inspector. A wry smile came across his lips.

Chapter 14

Macleod sat in the passenger seat as Hope drove the car back to the rather upmarket estate where the DCI's house was located. The day was grey, and it felt cold which in a lot of ways reflected Macleod's mood. Something needed to break, because at the moment everything they chased ended up with one of his team facing peril. Clarissa was okay and he thanked God for that, but he was getting sick of this.

The DCI was in some ways a punt in the dark, but he couldn't forget the fact that the man knew that Clarissa was going down to the borders. He knew about the address. He knew Winston Arnold. Somebody in the group they were chasing seemed to know where to be, when to close off possible leads, even if it meant taking out their own members.

'Look,' said Hope. 'Two cars in the drive. The wife must be in. Before when we went, he didn't want us to come in. Didn't want her involved in any of it. Seemed a little bit over the top. I mean, you might not want Jane in the room, but it doesn't stop you inviting colleagues into your house.'

'It's not uncommon,' said Macleod. 'I do try and shield Jane from a lot of what we do.'

'But it was me coming for a conversation, me looking for help at that time of the morning,' said Hope. 'Didn't feel right.'

Hope parked the car outside the front of the house, and they walked the driveway, past both vehicles to the front door where Macleod rapped loudly. Hope noted there was a doorbell but Macleod ignored it and rapped the door again instead.

'Hello,' said Lawson. 'Come in. How are the pair of you anyway? How are you holding up?'

'As well as we ever do,' said Macleod.

'Somebody told me that they tried to blow Clarissa up.'

'Who said that?' asked Macleod.

'Word from the station. I've still got a few people in there who like me. Although I think I kind of made a rod for my own back the way I treated you. Sorry for that, Seoras. I just got it completely wrong.'

'That you did,' said Hope.

'You did tell me,' said Lawson. 'But come. Come on in.'

'We see the missus is at home. Are you sure this is all right?' said Macleod.

'Of course, it is. She's just flittering about upstairs. We'll not disturb her. Don't need to bring any in front of her.'

'I understand,' said Macleod. They marched through to the front room.

'Just take a seat on the sofa,' said Lawson. 'Can I get you anything?' He stopped and looked at Macleod. 'Decent coffee, isn't it? Ross made you decent coffee. I don't think I'll have your type here.' The man seemed nervous, chattier and more welcoming than he'd ever done to Macleod before.

'Shall I come give you a hand?' asked Hope.

'No, no, no, you sit down there.' The man began to fuss and then walked out into the kitchen.

'Are you sure you're all right?' asked Macleod loudly when he heard something thump.

'I'm fine, Seoras. Just a second.' Lawson appeared at the door about a minute later. He came over and stood in front of the pair of them. 'There's no sugar in yours, is there, Macleod?' Macleod shook his head. 'What about you, Sergeant . . . sorry, Hope. First names, isn't it? Seoras and Hope. I forgot that.'

'No sugar for me,' said Hope, 'but if it's any trouble, I'll go make it. You can sit and talk to the inspector.'

'What would that look like? Two senior men sending out the woman to make the coffee. It's not a good look, is it?'

'You seem a bit on edge, Alan,' said Macleod.

'Can you blame me? I'm not exactly clear about the future after what happened, and here you are coming to talk to me in my own house. Makes you get kind of nervous.'

'There's no need to be. I'm only looking to talk to you about Winston Arnold. A few things when I was off.'

'Could Hope not sort that out for you?'

'Well, she wasn't running the investigation. Then, you remember, she got the bang on the head and it was down to Ross then. He's great, but he wasn't there to lead, was he?'

'Remarkable young man,' said Lawson, 'remarkable. But before we talk, I should really get the coffee.' He marched over towards the door, out through to the kitchen and then he stopped again, turned round, and looked at Hope.

'You really would suit the hair down. Do you realise that?' Hope looked inquisitively. 'Quite the officer,' said Lawson. 'You really are. I'll get the coffee.'

Macleod thought he almost lingered looking at her wistfully. Hope looked the other way and Macleod saw Lawson's head droop almost as if she'd rejected him. He sat with his hands folded while the man disappeared off into the kitchen.

Macleod could hear the coffee machine being switched on. It was filter coffee and it gurgled. At least it would be okay. Wasn't any of that instant stuff. It took about three minutes with the coffee machine gurgling before Macleod began to wonder where the former DCI was.

'You okay in there?' shouted Macleod.

Nothing came from the other room.

'I said, "Are you okay?"'

Again, nothing came to Macleod. He looked over at Hope who reflected the same concerned look. Then they heard a loud bang and a crack. Together they sprinted for the door. Hope, arriving first, let out a loud gasp, then informed Macleod of what had happened. He wasn't quite sure how, but when he turned and saw the chair lying on its back, and Lawson swinging from a rope tied up to the kitchen ceiling, the previous scene that he'd only heard was flashing before his eyes.

'Get the legs,' said Macleod.

Hope ran forward flinging her arms around the man's knees. She drove him up. Macleod grabbed the chair, lifting it back up, allowing Hope to put the weight of the legs back onto the chair. The man was still flopping, and she had to support his weight.

'I'll do it,' said Macleod. 'You get up on the chair, so you then get that rope off the ceiling.'

Macleod then shouldered up at the man's waist. It felt like the man was about to flop over, but something was supporting the upper body, presumably the rope from the ceiling. He saw Hope jump up on the chair and work busily above her head, and suddenly, the top half of the body fell onto Macleod. He struggled a bit with the weight, but as Hope jumped down, she was able to assist him with laying DCI Lawson on the kitchen floor. Macleod checked for a pulse. There was nothing. When he looked at the neck, it was snapped across.

'Call the ambulance,' said Macleod. 'I think he's gone but call it anyway.' He heard Hope press her mobile screen and then request an ambulance to the house. There was no breath from the DCI's body. The chest not rising and falling, the neck at an impossible angle.

'Two cars, Hope,' said Macleod. 'Two cars. He knew we were coming in. He planned this. He looked at you for one last time, looked at you and then . . . but there's two cars, Hope. Where's his wife?'

The pair stood up, ran out into the hall, and began shouting for Mrs Lawson. They ran round the lower floor of the house finding no one. Then Hope scrambled up the stairs ahead of Macleod. Hoped tore through the bedrooms and the bathroom, but couldn't find anything.

Macleod returned back down, looked at the body lying in the kitchen, and quickly began to search through it. As he reached the inside shirt pocket of Lawson, he found a piece of paper neatly folded. He took it out, opened it up, but saw there were no symbols, just simple, plain writing.

'Dear Seoras, I worked hard for them. Worked very hard and it will come to fruition. The plan was I would just leave, leave in disgrace, but that would've been okay, as the glory would come later and the Master would rise. Now with you coming, I can see it's my time. I was next on the list. Next to prepare a sacrifice. Out of the picture, you wouldn't have known it was me. With my time off, I'd even already abducted the child. It's done. You're too late and now all is ready. Tell

McGrath she could have hit the big time with me. She could have been on our side. She could have won, too.'

Macleod held the letter in front of him, his hands almost trembling. They'd been through the house. He knew they were coming.

'What is it, Seoras? What is it?'

He handed over the note to Hope, got up off his knees, and walked to the patio doors at the rear of the kitchen. As he opened them, he looked down the long garden, seeing a shed about halfway down with a summer house. Macleod began to walk with Hope chasing after him.

'What is it, Seoras? What is it?'

Macleod, eyes pinned forward, kept walking, looking at the glass door of the summer house. As he got closer, he could see something on the floor inside. Quickly, he opened the door, stepped inside, and looked at the figure of a small child with a bare back. At the centre of a mass of intricately carved symbols was an upside-down cross, almost mocking him. He went down to his knees, feeling like a weight was being borne on top of him. *No*, he thought. *No!*

His eyes closed briefly, taking him away from the sight. When he opened them again, he saw the dark hair at the back of the innocent child's head. Child, but one that had the look of a tortured soul on it. From behind him, he heard the gasp of McGrath and she knelt down beside them. 'Not your fault,' she said. 'Not your fault.'

'He nearly got Clarissa as well,' said Macleod. 'He nearly . . .' His fist swung out to the right, connecting with the wall and breaking part of the wood.

'Two cars,' she said, 'Seoras. Two cars.'

Hope stood up. Macleod watched her stalking around the

summer house, but it was one room. It had some chairs. It had a long sofa, like a little house. Soon she disappeared out of the door. Macleod stood up, began to call into the station, ready to advise them what had happened. He saw Hope walk to the shed.

'It's got a lock, Seoras. It's got a lock on it, but it's been opened. Why would he leave it open? Why would he do that? He had us come here. He . . .'

'He wants us to go in there,' said Macleod. 'He wants us to go in there. He played this from the start. He was their plant. He was the one, like a buffoon, like a laughing joker in front of us. I thought he was an idiot. He wasn't. He was just devious. Just . . .'

Hope entered the shed, calling to Macleod. He stepped around the small wooden door, watched as inside the shed, Hope opened the single door of the one cupboard on the left-hand side. As she did so, she had to step out of the way as the body of a woman crashed down, tipping up plastic buckets, knocking garden tools off the shelves.

'Do you know what she looked like?' asked Hope. 'Did you ever meet Mrs Lawson?'

'No,' said Macleod. 'But I think I just have.' He turned, walked out of the shed and did the only thing he could think of and reported the death to the station.

'This is Detective Inspector Macleod. I'll require full backup,' and he gave the address. 'I need a unit to contain the scene. I need forensics out. I've got three dead bodies.'

The voice on the other end was calm and took a moment before advising that help was on its way. As he closed down the call, Macleod looked around at the long garden, the small bridge that went over a tiny pond. It had the look of a happy house, a house like any other. Maybe it lacked children. Maybe that's why there was an ornamental pond.

Why? thought Macleod. *Why on earth would you want to bring something to wreck all of this, to destroy everyone else?* He had looked at Hope. Lawson had almost wished for her as if he could start again, but instead, he'd followed something else. Macleod heard his phone ring, looked down and saw it was Clarissa, and put the phone to his ear. 'Yes?'

'What's up, Seoras? I'm out and ready to go. You got anything for me?'

'You could say that. Yes. Some people would say that.'

Chapter 15

There was a soft spit of rain in the air that made everything that little bit colder. Macleod was standing in the garden of DCI Lawson's house, his coat on, and also a pair of gloves that Ross had thought to bring with him. The team were searching the household, assisting Jona, and also canvassing the neighbours to see if they'd noted anything in the previous days. Clarissa had hobbled around, but Macleod was struggling seeing her, reminded that she'd almost gone to her death in the borders.

As usual, she was living up to her name after taking a hit and was working as hard as anyone. He'd half a mind to stop her, to send her home, but he knew that would be sending her to a comfortable hell that she didn't want. She needed this. She needed to be out and about and doing, not sitting at home thinking about how she had nearly been blown sky high.

Jona Nakamura and her team were busy, white coverall suits combing the house looking for anything that might help narrow the investigation further. It was now nine o'clock at night, and Ross approached his inspector with an unsure look on his face.

'What's up, Ross?' asked Macleod.

'DCI's suicide's hit the press already. It's out online. Plenty of comment around it, too.'

'What do you mean?'

'It says you didn't screw up, sir,' said Ross. 'It said it was Lawson all along. Lawson got it wrong, but now that he's dead and you found another body, they're saying it was him, him that did it all. They're almost wrapping it up. Vindicating you, sir, but wrapping up.'

'Of course, they are, Ross. Don't you see? That's what this group are doing, lifting me up for the fall. There's all this symbology that's tied into their mindset. They're going to let me be lifted back up to crash back down again. As if killing seven more kids isn't bad enough, they have this thing about putting my career in tatters as well. Well, if they get the seven kids, the career's not going to matter much anyway.' He turned his back on Ross, who was going to say something but then obviously thought better of it.

'Are you all right, Seoras?' said a voice from the dark. Macleod looked over and Hope appeared from the other end of the garden. 'Just been checking to see if there was anything left about. What was Ross saying?'

'Says I'm vindicated. Apparently, Lawson was responsible for all of it, not just this child. Do we know yet where that child's come from?'

'Just heard. We've got a distraught single mother from up the road who wasn't even aware that her child had gone. That's how close she was to him.'

'Well, let's get somebody up there, interview her. Find out how this child disappeared. See if that will give us any clues into another one of the group.'

Macleod's phone began to ring, and he saw it was the

assistant chief constable.

'Jim. I'll have an update for you if you want.'

'I'm coming personally to get it, Seoras. I'm going to do a small briefing in front of Lawson's house. We have to answer this. There's a senior police officer involved. Papers are talking about how it's Lawson that's done everything. I want to try dispelling the belief that we've solved this just in case it goes wrong.'

'You might find that harder than you think,' said Macleod. 'He's got a suicide note to look like he's regretful. Killed his wife too, taking one last victim with him. I mean it's set up for the papers to lap up, isn't it?'

'I'll be with you at ten. I'm on the way in the car. Just don't come out front. I'll set up; I'll do it all. You keep going on the case.'

'You'll have a right rugby scrum to get through,' said Macleod. He'd taken a peep not long before and saw the mass of cameras and cars. He closed down the call as Clarissa hobbled up to him.

'Are you okay'? she said.

'It's good to see you,' said Macleod. 'Nearly lost you there.'

'It takes more than that to beat me,' she said. 'Don't fold on me now. We need to keep going; we need to get to the bottom of this.'

'How, what have we?' said Macleod 'What have we got left now? Winston's dead. Lawson's killed himself. We're looking for a man with a bust-up nose. That's the long and the short of it, and we haven't got anything from it. One of the problems is these people are too blooming good, Clarissa, backing themselves up. It's no wonder we couldn't trace anything with them knowing our every movement, Lawson being on top of it. Should have seen Lawson. I should have.'

'He's one of our own, and he's betrayed us,' said Clarissa. 'I get that. I so get that. I don't think he could hurt you in any other way in a more powerful fashion other than to take Jane away.'

'We should have seen it. Instead, I just went at the job. Keep trying to do this. Keep trying to . . .'

'Enough, Seoras,' said Clarissa. 'I'm not listening to this. We've got to scour this place. We've got to find something else to hang onto, something else to go at, because if we don't, we've got seven dead kids in our hands to top the five already gone.'

Macleod tried to raise his head, but there was no doubting how crestfallen he was. Clarissa reached forward and simply hugged him.

'I don't think that's truly appropriate at the moment, Sergeant,' he said.

'Shut up. You need this. Sometimes you need a bit of help too. Come on. What's next? Think. You need to think.'

Hope returned. 'Everything all right?'

'Just having a moment,' said Clarissa. 'Need to know what to do next. Need to know where to go.'

'Well, we hunt,' said Hope. 'Ross traces through computers, whatever he can do. We go back over our tracks, we see if there's anything else, and we look for a man with a broken nose until something else breaks. I'm not sure what good that's going to be.'

'It's quite defeatist,' said Clarissa.

'And also, standard police work,' said Hope. Clarissa nodded and walked off, limping.

'Well,' Macleod said, 'she needs to be pointed, needs to be

told what to do, where to go after. Brutal when she knows where she's going.'

'Where do we go beyond that?' said Hope. 'Laid it all out for you. Do you have any other suggestions?'

'No,' said Macleod as he heard a shout from the rear of the house.

'Inspector, the Assistant Chief Constable's here. He'd like a word with you.' Macleod nodded, turned away from Hope, and trudged up to the rear of the house. He entered the kitchen, bypassing the forensics who were still working, and sat down in the front room alongside Jim.

'Challenging times,' said Jim in the understatement of the year.

'One of us, Jim, one of us. One of us was involved with them. One of us they set to die, one of us just carved symbols into a kid, one of us killed his wife. Us, Jim. I know we've had bad apples over the time, but not this.'

'Easy,' said Jim. 'I'd kick you out of the situation, but I need that brain. I need that brain to find who's doing this, why it's happened, how it's happened. Your mind is capable of that, Macleod. You know that, Seoras, as well as I do. Your agitation is because they're beating you at the moment. They're beating you; they're beating us all.'

'You ever worked a case like this?' asked Macleod.

'I worked a longer one. When I was in Hong Kong, I worked four months of every two weeks a child dying,' said Jim. 'I found the bloke because he managed to drop half a matchbox one night at a station getting onto the tube which was spotted by some other little kid. That was between many more dying. Sometimes it takes luck, Seoras. Sometimes it takes a mistake. I take it you had no luck trying to trace down Samuel Forbes or Karen Whitelaw?'

'None, not a trace has been seen of them. Ross has been poring through CCTV here, there, and everywhere but it's like a needle in a haystack. They could be anywhere.'

'With Winston blown up, we're looking for a packet of matches left in the subway,' said Jim. 'That's where we are. That's not your fault. That's not my fault. That's nobody's fault. It's just what is and what is, is what is, Seoras. Remember that. "What is" is always "what is". It's not a case that we get to pick and choose how easy or difficult something's going to be. You're at the head of this because if there's something small, you'll get it. Don't quit on me, don't go under. Get out in front of this. I'm about to go and talk to the press. I'm going to have to go and tell them that one of ours is involved, that one of ours let kids die. You were right; there's no other path for me to go on than to front this—make sure you do, too.'

The Assistant Chief Constable stood up, placed a hand on Macleod's shoulder. 'I don't need to tell you we're depending on you on this one. More than that, seven kids are. Whatever I can do, whatever, Seoras.'

'You're taking the vultures on to begin with,' he said. 'That's plenty to begin with.'

Jim departed to the front of the house and Hope came running to Macleod. 'Seoras, I got something; come on.'

Macleod stood up quickly, paced out of the house and down the garden towards the shed. As he approached, Jona stepped out and shouted over one of her colleagues to grab some white suits.

'I don't want to disturb this too much. I'll try and get a photograph of it for you.'

'Of what?' asked Macleod.

'There's a note inside the underwear of Mrs Lawson.'

'The underwear?'

'Stuffed inside her bra; it looks like a rush job. She may have found something. It's maybe why she was killed. Maybe he was worried.'

'Maybe he's just taking her with him,' said Hope, 'if you want to try and second-guess this lot.'

'What does it say?' asked Macleod.

'Suit up and you can find out,' said Jona, stepping back inside the shed.

Two minutes later, Macleod was dressed in the coverall and with Hope walked into the shed. It was distinctly more cramped and lit up by some of the strongest lights Macleod had ever endured at this distance. Carefully, Jona, in full overalls and mask, was removing a piece of paper from inside Mrs Lawson's bra.

'You wouldn't pop something in here,' said Jona, 'unless you were hiding it and had to hide it quickly.'

She pulled open the paper and revealed it to be an A5 sheet. On the paper, written in pencil, were a large number of symbols. It lasted three lines. Jona looked over at Macleod.

'Are they the symbols that you had to decode for?' she asked.

'They are,' he said, and took out his phone.

'What are you doing?' asked Hope.

'Ross put them on here for me in case I lost them. Now, hang on, let's have a look at this.'

Hope could see the man becoming more alive. Suddenly, the detective vein took over and he worked through the code in front of him.

'What does it say, Seoras?' asked Hope, but the inspector put his hand up.

122

'Easy,' he said, 'I'm working on it.' He stopped thirty seconds later, walked out of the shed, breathing heavily.

'As far as I can gather, this appears to be . . . I have an address here,' he said. 'I'm having difficulty translating the word up at the top. Possibly some sort of base, but also one that's live at the moment. Maybe it was where Lawson was meant to run. I don't know, but what I do know is his death's been run by the papers. Maybe they'll not be there. Maybe they've tidied up. We've got a couple of hours. I say we go see what this place is.'

'You think it could be another trap?' asked Hope.

'No,' said Macleod. 'There's nothing to say she was involved. I go with Jona's idea. The note was quickly tucked away; she found something she didn't want to. I think the woman has done us a favour, Hope. I think it's time to go and make sure that we repay that favour by making sure nobody else gets hurt.'

Chapter 16

Macleod's decode gave an address that was a warehouse in Inverness, tucked away on a little-used estate. From the outside, the building looked derelict, but it had a relatively new lock on a wire gate. Taking no chances, Macleod had brought along armed police to infiltrate the building first of all, before any of his officers would go inside. He'd also brought sniffer dogs to check for explosives around the area in case this was just one more dirty trap. As he stood with Hope beside him, Macleod watched as the figures moved back and forward, breaking in through the gate, then disappearing inside the building.

It was extremely dark, large floodlights illuminating most of the ground around the warehouse, but the inside would be even darker until the armed squads had declared it all to be safe. It took fifteen minutes in the cold before Macleod was approached by the leader of the infiltration team and advised that the area was safe. Macleod thanked him, motioned his team to follow and walked through the wire gates onto the concrete beyond. Here and there it was pitted where the rain had worn it away, and Macleod wondered how long this place had been here. Most of the wire fencing was rusty.

As he approached the solid-enough-looking door, he realised that the infiltration team had managed to put the power on, giving light inside. A white corridor lay before Macleod, with paint stripped back, mould setting in along the walls. It stank, and Macleod wandered down it until he saw another door at the end that reminded him of the flat where Ian Lamb had wet the inside to create mould to keep others out. It made him a clever hidey-hole to continue his observations on Amanda Hughes, the single mother who had died in the first attack.

Macleod stepped inside a large hall, one side of which had a highly decorated wall. Other walls seemed to be covered in graffiti, maybe from an earlier time. There were a few tables and chairs in front of the more artistic wall, and Macleod could see that several formed a semicircle. Possibly a place for meetings. He counted the chairs; there were twelve.

'I think that's far enough, Inspector,' said a voice over his shoulder. Macleod turned and saw Jona.

'Of course, you're right,' he said. 'Everyone, back up.' Almost as quickly as they'd gone in, the small team backed away, and Jona approached with her team.

As soon he'd exited though, Macleod got a hold of Hope and insisted she suit up with him, both donning their coveralls, covering their feet, and re-approaching the building. Once inside the large hall again, Macleod stood looking at the mural.

'That's quite something, isn't it?' said Hope. 'It's beautiful in some ways, and yet the pictures are gross.'

In the middle of the mural were seven people, each holding a child and placing a knife into each of them. Other parts of the mural saw a land that was being covered with a pestilence, disease, wrath, anarchy raging in cities, yet the left-hand side showed an almost paradise, which quickly blended into the horror of the rest.

'It's telling the tale, isn't it?' said Macleod. 'That's the way things are, although I think that's an exaggeration. That's the killing of the kids and in this, darkness sweeps across the land.'

'It's very bold,' said Hope. 'This would've taken time. They must have been meeting here.'

'For a long time. We'll get Ross to check out who owns it, see if we're getting links through that. Gather up the team to canvas the area. I know there's not many houses about, but you never know what people have seen. Any lead we can get at the moment is going to help because, otherwise, well, this is it. I doubt Jona is going to get anything. They've been too well drilled before.'

'You going to stand there all day?' asked Jona.

'Where do you want me to stand?' requested Macleod.

'Well, you can gawk at that picture from anywhere,' she said.

'Don't you see it?' said Macleod. 'This is prophecy. This is someone putting the idea out there. The power of this is incredible. The fact they actually convinced eleven other people to come with them on this. We're not talking about a single murderer or somebody self-obsessed, somebody who can do all the minor details. They've got to coordinate eleven other people and all the difficulties that come with that.'

'And,' said Hope, 'one convinced so much that he committed suicide as well as killing his own wife.'

Macleod saw a figure, a face on the side that contained the pestilence. You had to almost look through the picture to see it. It was a representation of what he would've called the devil, and it sent a chill through him.

'Just remember,' said Jona, 'it is what it is, a painting. We can take a brush and just wash that down.'

'It's more than a painting,' said Macleod. 'It's not even an idea, to them it's a reality. These are people who are actually obsessed enough, who are convinced enough that this will happen, that they'll do whatever.'

'I don't get it,' said Jona. 'What's the reward in all this?'

'That's true,' said Hope. 'Usually when you're watching the films and stuff, anyone that's sort of going along with the devil, that is usually because they're going to get more power, or they're going to get this, that, or whatever. They're always looking for something, making a shady deal.'

'That's just a film. These people are not actors; these people are the real deal.'

'What?' asked Jona. 'You think this will come to pass?'

'I didn't say that. I said these people are the real deal. They are true believers. In my side of the church, you get people who are overzealous. They believe they know it all. They believe they understand it. Therefore, what they see is right and they do what they do because that is right to them, and they won't be swayed by it. This is the same.'

'I don't get you,' said Jona. 'How can you feel it's right to kill kids?'

'Some have anger against something, against society. Maybe each of them has got a different pain, but it unites in this, this thing that will change. Those who want to do good, they think that as long as you do whatever in the right way, it'll happen. These people think the same thing. They're trying to change everyone else with an external force. I get why devil worshipers, or whatever these people are, would fall for it.'

'What do you mean?' asked Hope.

'Well,' said Macleod, 'we never get asked to change everybody

127

else. We only ever get asked to change ourselves.' They stayed in silent contemplation, while Hope stepped back with Jona. He could hear them whispering.

'I'm not nuts. I'm getting inside their head. Unfortunately, I see people that are close to this mark in other walks of life too.'

Footsteps cut across the concrete floor and Macleod heard them out of uniform step, almost alike the clip of a horse's trot.

'Nice of you to join us,' said Macleod.

'Have you ever tried to get a coverall over a shawl?' asked Clarissa, and then she stopped and stared. 'That detail's amazing,' she said. 'This is no amateur. This has been done by somebody good.'

'Maybe we can get someone to find out who did it?' suggested Macleod. 'Can't be that many people could produce a masterpiece like this. Not on this scale, done on the quiet.'

'I'll get on it,' said Clarissa, 'but I think we should go and get Abby to look at the picture. This is telling a story. There might be stuff in this that she would be able to understand because this mural wasn't for us, was it?'

'I don't think so,' said Macleod. 'I think this is for them. I think this is a rallying call. I think this is the focal point they come back to, and I think you're right, Clarissa. There might be something in this. Get Abby now.'

Clarissa ignored how abrupt he was with his comment and hobbled back off.

Macleod didn't move in the next forty-five minutes that it took Abby to arrive. Only when he heard the sharp click of two-inch heels across the floor did he turn around. Jona had made a path that had been checked over and escorted the woman to a standing point along with Macleod. He did notice that her brunette hair had been tied up and covered with a net.

'Well, I don't feel the most attractive in this get-up, Inspector, but I do give you thanks for bringing me. That is stunning, truly stunning.'

'What does it mean? Is there anything in this?' asked Macleod. 'Is there anything in this ungodly work that you can actually use?'

'Give me a minute,' she said. He noticed she had a rucksack on, and watched as she took it off, unzipped it, and brought out several pieces of paper.

'Bits and pieces I've collected over the years from the right sort of manuscript that's going to help us here. You can see there's an obvious basic interpretation. The idea that the world's okay, but kill seven kids and suddenly the world is a very bad place. Can you see the face?'

'If you look through the right-hand side of it, yes,' said Macleod. 'It's . . .'

'Disturbing. You ever seen that face painted anywhere else?' asked Abby.

'No,' said Macleod. 'You?'

'I'm not surprised,' she said. 'He hasn't been portrayed like that in a long while.'

'I take it, it's the devil?'

'Well, that's one name for him,' said Abby, 'but let's not focus on that face too much. Let's have a look at the other clues.'

'What do you mean, other clues?'

'The stars in the heavens, they are not our stars,' said Abby. 'Those stars come from this page here,' and she pulled a page across to Macleod. 'Other stars have burnt out to be replaced by these ones, movement in the heavens. It's very hard to explain but it's a change that causes a lot of this or so they think.'

'Where do you stand on this?' asked Macleod. 'Do you think this is real? Do you think this is something that shouldn't be trifled with? Or do you think it's all just larks by fools?'

'Where do you stand, Inspector, before you ask me?'

'Well, I think evil's very real wherever it comes from, be it a fallen angel or just the heart of a man or a woman, but it's very real.'

'I'll join you in that,' said Abby. 'I don't go with all of this, that by this occurring, pestilence will follow, et cetera, et cetera. I do, however, believe that some people do and they will follow this.'

'This is a murder investigation,' said Macleod. 'When you talk to my team, please deliver it in that form. Anything you can help us to get to these children before this happens to them. That's how we operate. Don't give them anything beyond that. They're spooked enough by it. I've nearly lost all three of them at some point or other.'

'Of course, Inspector. I take it you can see the symbol at the heart. It's very cleverly interlaid but if you're looking for it . . .'

'You're talking about the upside-down cross laid out by nature,' said Macleod. 'I saw it. Some of the rest of my team didn't.'

'It's an old way of saying that the common order would be subverted. That what was made wasn't right, wasn't good, that somebody else should be stepping forward to take the place of it. I'm going to take some time on this, Inspector. If I was you I wouldn't stand here with me. The thing about works like this is they affect the mind, your dreams, what comes after. It's probably just clever artwork that does it or maybe it's the possibilities that lie within the drawing that makes your mind go that way. Go catch these people. Go chase your other leads. I take it you have something else; you're not just relying on me.'

'We traced one of the people involved in this,' said Macleod. 'This goes no further. DCI Lawson kicked me off the investigation, committed suicide, previously having killed another child, cut the symbols, and dispatched his own wife. His wife had hidden a note in code which brought us here. Ross is now checking his computers. Jona has her team over there as well going through that house, and we're pretty stretched trying to work out anything else. Everybody I know has gone to ground, except for a man with a busted nose, who I can't seem to find anywhere now, but he kept turning up all the time previously. So, Abby, please understand me when I say you're not the only lead I've got, but you're probably the best one at the moment. Take your time please, get it right, but find me something in here. Find me what it means to them. Find me the story.'

He watched as she sat down on her backside, folded her legs in front of her while he watched the two-inch stiletto heels poke out either side. 'Give me space.'

Macleod left the building, returning out to his car to stand and look back. As he did so, Ross appeared with a coffee in hand. Macleod drank it eagerly, but was fighting to keep the chill from inside, from ideas racing up to his mind.

Chapter 17

Macleod sat at his desk fuming, as he noted that none of the team had popped in in the last twenty minutes. This was because a young constable had delivered the daily paper to him, and the front headline had a picture of the mural. *Things were hard enough without having people undercut you*, thought Macleod. *Where did it come from?*

'Clarissa, get in here.'

The door opened and Clarissa hobbled in. 'They might call me the Rottweiler, but I don't come to heel. I'll thank you to be a bit more polite than that.'

'Sorry,' said Macleod. 'It's just this flaming picture that's in the papers. How'd they get a picture of the mural? We only just discovered it. It's literally the following morning, and now we have it, a picture in the papers. What press person in their right mind runs that? Look at it.'

'I've been looking at it, done nothing but look at it,' said Clarissa. 'Gone over and over it with Abby but at the moment, she's still working away on it.'

'Well, are you sure it didn't come from her?'

Macleod saw Clarissa give him a scowl that would have turned anyone else cold. 'You can tell me when I've done a bad job, but don't you ever come after my integrity, and integrity of people that I vouch for. Get a hold of yourself, Seoras. This is getting to you.'

Macleod stood up, turned, and did his familiar, looking-out-of-the-window routine. The morning was cold but crisp. 'Yes, it is,' he said. 'It's getting to all of us. We need an end to this. We need the right end.'

'That's a bit reflective for you.'

Macleod spun around. 'Well, what do you expect? We started out facing horrific scenes. We had to work in ways and means that we never wanted to work in. I've seen the three of you nearly killed. I've nearly been killed myself. If we get to the end and we haven't saved those poor little souls, how is it going to leave us? Huh? It isn't going to leave us.'

'We did all we can,' said Clarissa.

'Maybe, but it's not enough.'

'What else would you have us do? Abby will find something. Abby is good, really good.'

'Well, you find me where this came from. Get hold of the blasted Echo. I don't care if they say it's a protected source. You sort them.'

'I will do, but you quiet down,' said Clarissa. 'Somebody like Ross doesn't have the shoulders I have. He doesn't have the guts to turn around and give you a kick back. You watch your team.'

As she turned away, hobbling through the door, and then closing it with a loud slam, Macleod knew she was right. He sat back down, took his coffee cup in hand, placed it to his lips, and found it to be completely cold. *Haven't been that long since somebody brought one in*, he thought. *Surely it hasn't.*

He stared out through the windows to the office beyond and

he could read the fatigue on the shoulders of his staff. Even those that were just there to assist, brought onto the team, seemed to be weary. In particular, he looked over at Ross. It seemed like the man didn't sleep and yet he was still chasing through that application, still waiting to hear if he would have a child.

That was where it all began, thought Macleod, and then that child had been brought into it. He wondered how that made Ross feel, if he had second thoughts then. Jane had come under fire several times because of the job. Hope's John had too. This was the thing—you wanted to keep them safe; you did your best but sometimes, things were taken out of your hands.

Macleod watched Ross answer the phone and his face almost became elated, and then Ross jumped up, almost running over to the office door, bursting through but recovered himself to knock first.

'Come in,' said Macleod. Ross arrived at his desk, almost out of breath. 'Got something, boss. Got something. I took Lawson's computer down to our geeks and they've got into it. They found an address on the dark web, an address for Dark Union, the group we think's at the core of this.'

'Let's go then,' said Macleod. 'Whereabouts is it?'

'It's on the web, sir. It's a web address. We found a web address.'

'Okay,' said Macleod. 'So that helps me, how?'

'Working on that bit. Going to see if we can trace it back to a physical address. See who put it up there, who adds to the site, who works on it.'

'So, you're going to get me a proper address from this?' said Macleod.

Ross suddenly looked dejected again, his shoulders dropped.

'We're going to do our best to find an address. It might not be the address of any of the group members, it might be a hosting company, it could be a number of things, but it's a link and it's something to chase and it's what my people are doing and given what else we've got and the timeframe, yes, it's a shot in the dark in some ways but it's a good shot.'

The man turned and started to walk away.

'Ross, stop. Sorry, I'm just up against it,' said Macleod. 'The whole thing is getting to me. I feel like we can't get a grip. They close everything down.'

'Well, they didn't close this down,' said Ross. 'This is very much open, wide open. I'm surprised he didn't get rid of the computer, really surprised he didn't.'

'I don't think he had time,' said Macleod. 'His wife had that note on her. I think he killed her deliberately not long before we got out there. Jona will probably corroborate that. He knew I was coming to see him. He knew I had an idea he might be involved. He was the next up to kill a kid.'

'We got where the kid came from?'

'Yes,' said Macleod. 'Five doors up. I don't think it was the kid they were after but five doors up is a divorced mum. Last couple of months has been on her own.'

'He just went and grabbed a kid?'

'That's what I'm saying. We found the mum, hands tied up in a cupboard in their own house. Neighbours said they were concerned to one of our police officers, said that they hadn't seen them about, and our kid hadn't gone to school with them that morning. Then there was nobody at the house. We were down the road. She asked the question. We looked into it.'

Ross hung his head down.

'There's a lot of black here, lot of dark stuff,' said Macleod.

135

'But you've done well. You're coming through on angles I can't do,' said Macleod. 'You know computers and I don't get on. You're doing well, Ross.'

'We need to get better. We need to get there before them.'

'Just keep pushing. Let me worry about the time scales. You keep pushing.'

Macleod sat at his desk, going through previous statements, looking through the earlier killings, trying to work out if he'd missed anything. Hope came through, gave him a report on what each part of the team were doing and how they were getting on. She also updated that there was no sign of Samuel Forbes or Karen Whitelaw, despite every police officer in the force now having had their picture placed with them. They had truly gone underground.

As Macleod listened to his sergeant go through all that was being done, he saw lines on her face that he never realised were there before. There was the scar that she had received from saving his Jane, the acid that had burnt the face, but closer to the eyes he could see the wrinkles coming. Long hours, no sleep, worry about the next victim. It all contributed to the way his face now looked. He didn't think he was ugly, just worn, like a kitchen appliance that had been in use for twenty years. You look at it, you think it's a good old warhorse, but it's not the look of a brand-new kitchen.

'That's about it, Seoras. You okay with all that? Seoras? Are you even there?'

'Yes, I'm here. You said . . . sorry. Makes you have some retrospection, doesn't it? Cases like this makes you realise how people have changed, what it does to us.' He looked at Hope.

'What? I was sat here, and you looked at me and you thought, what?'

'I thought, "What a tremendous job you've done,"' said Macleod.

'If you're going to lie, at least make it vaguely convincing,' said Hope. 'What were you thinking?'

He thought he might say, 'You're still a beautiful woman,' but that could be taken in a rather creepy fashion. When they'd started off, he had felt a lot of things around her, for her, and though now they were good friends and thoroughly professional, it wasn't something he wanted to bring back up. But he couldn't tell her that what she did wore on her.

'You look weary as anything,' she said. 'I imagine I do too. If you want to tell me how this job has affected me, how I don't look like I did when you first met me, that's fine,' she said. 'Because I don't. You don't have to worry about my opinion of myself. I can still turn a head when I want to. Knuckle down, Seoras; that's what you would say to me.'

He gave a smile, and she stood up and looked over at his coffee cup. 'I'll get Ross to make you some more.'

'Leave Ross alone. I'll come and do it myself,' he said, but the door barged open. It had to be Clarissa. Everybody else knocked. She had Abby in tow.

'Sit back down,' said Clarissa, and she spun about and hobbled over to the round table, pulling two chairs from it and almost throwing them into position beside Hope.

'First off, Seoras, that mural picture came to the Echo in the post. I chewed him out for it, told him he was an idiot for putting it in the copy, but apparently, ads have been down recently. He needs the sales to go up and the usual thing. Anyway, there's no trace back from that; got the envelope. I've sent it to forensics, but let's face it, that's not happening. Secondly, Abby's got something for you.'

137

Macleod stared over at the younger woman, dressed in rather gothic fashion. She had a long leather coat on this time, boots up to her knees, black jeans, a black t-shirt underneath and a golden cross dangling around her neck. Macleod looked at it and wondered if it was just an ornament to her, but the hunger got him.

'What do you have?' he asked.

'Well, Inspector, have you got a picture of the mural?'

Macleod pulled one from his desk, placed it down and Abby leant over with him, the cross dangling down between the pair of them. Her finger moved across to the far-right corner to the side depicting the hellfire to come. 'Can you see this swirl of letters?'

'No,' said Macleod.

'It's on the horn of that demon.'

'I can just about see a horn.'

'Well, if you blow it up or you look at the original, there's a pattern. Well, not a pattern, it's actual writing. It comes from an old script. A script mainly forgotten now.'

'It's not demon writing, is it?' asked Macleod.

'Well, it is linked into that and it's from a culture that's not around anymore. The thing is, the only known examples of it come from the medieval times and therefore we don't even know if they're accurate, but this picture mural is probably based on those times and the writings from them. We have been able to decode it, been able to take the symbols and . . .'

'And what?'

'Well, they work on a different calendar because no Satanic group is going to look at Anno Domini here.'

'And?' said Macleod.

'Let the woman have time to explain. She's done a lot of

work in this,' said Clarissa.

Macleod's hand went up. 'Shush. What, Abby? What?'

'Basically, you've got two days, Inspector, two days until they plan to do this.'

There was a knock on the door and Ross ran in again, panting. 'I've got it, sir. I've got it.'

'Not now, Ross. Just a second.'

'But I've got it.'

'Two days, Inspector,' said Abby.

'Are you sure?' asked Macleod.

'Of course, she's sure,' said Clarissa, 'I told you, don't question my sources, the people I bring in.'

'Shush,' said Macleod, and he held his hand up to Clarissa. He flicked his head over to Ross. He was standing looking like a child that needed the toilet. 'What have you got?' asked Macleod.

'The web address, we looked into it. We looked at who was accessing, who was putting it up there. It's gone through different routes, different country servers, too many to mention, but I've traced it to a house in Inverness. I've got you that address.'

Macleod looked up at his team. 'Magic.' he said, 'The lot of you, I could nearly kiss you.'

Chapter 18

The sunlight of a cold day tore through the window of the car, warming Macleod's chin and jaw as he stared at the traffic in front of him. Hope was navigating well, mainly due to the police car in front of her which was clearing the route with its blue lights and siren. He could feel the adrenaline rushing up inside. This was it. This is what he'd been longing for. It was like he had got a hold of the tail. They were thrashing. They were trying to throw you off. This is when the struggle began.

When he'd been brought up in the Isle of Lewis, he'd gone fishing at Holm, where his wife had died many years later. He remembered when the mackerel caught the line and you felt the tug, how the adrenaline kicked in as you fought with it to bring it back ashore, lift it out, and then finally bop it on the head with a mace. You extinguished its life before taking it home.

He remembered the struggle. Cases could be like this. You spent all the time not getting anywhere. Thinking you saw a little something you could delve into; it was like casting your line out into the sea. You thought you saw movement here. You thought you saw movement there, or you saw no movement at all and just cast it somewhere to stir the water up. But when they caught, when you got your teeth into something, when it bit, then you went for it.

'Really?' asked Hope. 'You could really kiss us all? I'm not sure that's today's way of addressing the team. I think 'Good job, everyone; now let's get cracking' would've been a much more considered response.'

'Shut up,' said Macleod.

'You're alive again. You can sense it, can't you?'

'Can you?' said Macleod. He wondered how she could drive so well while engaging in the conversation. She was better than him at driving, especially these days as he was getting a little rusty. Sometimes he forgot to check that mirror. Sometimes he drifted but then he was an Inspector. Nothing wrong with being driven around.

'It might be nothing though. It's just an address. It's just a . . .'

'No,' said Macleod. 'This is it. I can feel the tug of it. This is it. Two days. Hope, two days. I could kiss you all. You've all done well.'

'Even Clarissa?'

'Don't go there,' said Macleod. 'That's not funny. It's not funny.'

'I find it funny.'

'Yes, but she's serious. Clarissa needs someone. You can see that. At least she thinks she does.'

'Do we know who lives there?' asked Hope, changing the conversation.

'I haven't heard yet. Ross just gave the address, and we went.'

'Thankfully,' said Hope, 'no kisses.'

He flicked his eyes over at her. This was a lull before that moment when you got there, when you had to do. There wasn't really much else to discuss at the moment. They didn't know anything about the address, who would be there, what involvement they would have. The drive was just that, dead time before the next installment.

A cavalcade of cars pulled up in front of a small flat in the Inverness old town area. Macleod watched as a small team of armed officers knocked on the door before smashing it in. They raced through the building while Macleod stood outside; he thought this might be unnecessary. He thought it would be a heck of a trap with all the computer involvement, but after what had happened previously, he was taking no chances. When the head of the squad came down and advised Macleod that he needed to come up, he knew they'd found something. Two floors up, in one of a series of flats, Macleod found a petite Indian man on his knees with his face down to the carpet.

'Is he armed?' asked Macleod.

'No, he's been in that position since we came into the room.'

'Then please make sure he is unarmed, and we'll take it from there. Thank you, Sergeant.'

Two minutes later, the Indian man was sitting on a seat in the room. Macleod perched on a table beside him with Hope close by.

'What's your name?' asked Macleod.

'Sanjay,' said the man.

'What do you do here, Sanjay?'

The man looked at him. 'Computer.'

'Okay, you do computers. For whom?' The man looked at him blankly. 'Do you speak English?' Asked Macleod.

'English. Very good.'

'Where do you come from?' asked Macleod. The man simply

smiled back.

'I'll get a translator,' said Hope.

'What language?'

'Indian. He looks Indian to me,' said Hope.

'Yes. What language?'

Ross put his head in through the door of the room. 'Excuse me, sir. Got a moment?'

'What is it, Ross?'

'Found the workstation where he operates from downstairs. It's a good piece of kit. I'd like to know how he exactly did it.'

'That's going to be hard,' said Macleod. 'I'm not sure he speaks English.'

'Do you want me to set up a translation?'

'Do you speak Indian or whatever language it is?'

'No,' said Ross, 'but I know people who do. Hang on a minute.' Macleod watched Ross pull out his phone and dial up a number. He then spoke quietly to someone before approaching the man. 'I am Ross. Okay? Speak your language.'

The man looked blankly at him. Ross looked around and found lying around a set of instructions for building furniture. On the back of them, was a list of guarantees written in many languages. Ross held it in front of the man pointing to the English.

'This is mine,' he said. 'Ross, English. You?'

'Sanjay,' said Hope.

'Sanjay, which?' Ross ran his hand around the various languages to indicate the man should pick one. He watched the man take the brochure from him, staring at it, and then pointed.

'Read that one,' said Ross.

The man started off in a language that Ross didn't know.

'Hindi,' said a voice on the other end of Ross's phone.

'Are they listening?' asked Macleod.

'Quiet sir, please. Quiet,' said Ross. Ross started a brief conversation with the person on the phone and then stopped and turned to Macleod.

'With your permission sir, I want to take Sanjay downstairs and I want to talk to him. I'll find out for you what's happening. Can you give me twenty minutes?'

'Of course.' Macleod watched the pair disappear downstairs and then Hope smiled at him.

'He's some operator,' she said. 'I've never used that language line yet. He looks like he's practised it.'

'Well, it is Ross,' he said. 'Hopefully, he can find out what the man knows. I'll bring him in for questioning as well afterwards. Get an in-person translator.'

'That's because you don't like the phones,' said Hope. Macleod couldn't deny it. He didn't like talking over the phone when he could have somebody beside him, especially with translation. He needed someone you could look in the eye, someone you could clarify things with.

'Main thing is,' said Macleod, 'we need to know how he got contacted, why he is doing this. Is he part of the group?'

'Does he look like part of the group?' asked Hope.

He stood up and began pulling out the drawers of the room across the number of desks and tables. Everywhere was what Macleod would've described as computer junk cables. Those towers that housed the computers these days, large screens. There were mice everywhere, most of them wireless. Even the posters in the room showed diagrams of computer circuitry as far as Macleod could work out or was it a web network? He was rubbish at this thing. Hope disappeared and came back ten minutes later.

'There's a bed upstairs but it is basically a bed. There's a couple of photographs of some kids and a what looks like maybe a wife or girlfriend.'

'Maybe they brought him here?'

'Maybe. I think we need to speak to Ross for that.'

Ross returned with the man ten minutes later and had him sit down on a chair with a cup of coffee. *Where had he got the coffee from?* thought Macleod.

'Sanjay. His name is Sanjay Patel and he's come from India to try and earn some money. His family are quite poor; for whatever reason, he didn't seem to be able to earn a lot there, but he does have a brother in Bradford. He travelled there, then put in an advert looking for work. He was taken up by a man who he never met, all done by emails. When they chatted across the net, the other end came up with an avatar on the screen. We'll get into that, see where that goes but it could take time.

'He's basically worked to set up and monitor communications for this group and also to set up their website. I don't think he understands that it's an illegal group or certainly doesn't understand what's behind what they're doing. They told him that they needed a website on the dark web to be found only by those who can enjoy the topics the group engaged in because the things engaged in were extreme. He's a little bit shocked to find out they could be tied to these murders.' Macleod looked at the man. He could see he'd been crying.

'He's been very forthcoming, said Ross. He's told us all he knows I think but I'm not sure how much he does know. He's never met these people. This building has been given to him.

We'll try and work out what's happening with that because somebody's got to be paying for it or own it. The other thing is he has an address for correspondence. He asked for that, demanded it of them.'

'Correspondence, in what way.'

'He wanted somewhere to send things if he needed to. He said the trouble with a web address was he could have been dealing with people anywhere and then if things went wrong here, he was stuck in this country and maybe nobody else was.'

'So, he thought there was something illegal going on,' said Macleod.

'It's because it's on the dark web,' said Ross. 'He thought he should protect himself. He got an address for correspondence, and he checked it. He sent something to it and got a reply.'

'Where is it?'

'Bonar Bridge, not far away.'

Macleod looked over at Hope. 'On my way,' she said; give me the full address, Ross.'

'Hope, try to be discreet but take the armed team with you. We can't mess about; there's no time for surveillance. We need to get in there, get what we can from that address.'

'Will do,' said Hope. She pulled on her leather jacket and left the room. Macleod turned to look at Sanjay who had his hands up on his head. He stood up stumbling towards Macleod.

'Sorry. So sorry. I . . .'

Macleod put his hands up in front to try and protect himself, to try to push him back towards his chair. 'This building, Ross. I want to know who owns it and I think we'll take Mr. Patel in for some questioning.'

'I think he's innocent,' said Ross.

'He knew what he was doing wasn't right,' said Macleod. 'I

think we'll see what level of innocence comes through.'

Chapter 19

Macleod returned to the office, leaving Ross to sort through the computers and various technical items at the flat. Mr Patel had been brought in for interview and Macleod would have to wait for a live translator rather than one on the phone. He was not happy with this, but Mr Patel was being cooperative. Macleod had wanted Patel brought in as much for the man's safety as anything else. Being left out in the open, and given the track record that this group had, he was liable to end up dead. Dark Union didn't mess about with any members, considering them a liability when compromised.

As he stood around the office, Macleod was waiting to hear from Hope and the team he'd sent north to Bonar Bridge. A large part of him had got excited, but something else had bit back at him. He had hoped that instead of finding Mr Patel and his technical setup, they'd have found somebody within the group. Patel clearly wasn't that. Unlike other houses they'd been to, there was no occult material, nothing to connect the man to anything Satanic. Possibly his ethnicity was a problem on that front as well.

Macleod hadn't asked him, but maybe the man was a Hindu

with how many gods. He found it hard to believe Patel picked up being a Satanist from that sort of background. A lot of this was conjecture, and Macleod knew it.

His biggest problem was that they were now depending on racing to another building for another lead, a lead that basically was a drop-off point for post. As the team were all out, Macleod had made his own coffee and drank it as he looked out the window. At times, people thought he was just absent-minded, but in truth, he worked hard and probably best when there was nothing in front of him, letting the mind churn over. Part of him wished he had something to do because he was getting tense, waiting for Hope's call.

The phone went and Macleod jumped to it, putting it up to his ear. 'Hope. What have we got?'

'Inspector, this is Jona. I'd like you to come back over to Lawson's house.'

'I can't, Jona. I'm waiting for an important call from Hope. I'll be there as soon as I can afterwards.'

'No, I think you should come immediately. This may bust the case wide open.'

'What do you mean?' asked Macleod.

'When we came into the house, a member of my team noticed that one of the interior walls wasn't sealed up correctly. It had an access point. When we examined that point and we stripped back the entire wall, we found correspondence from this group for many years. There are hundreds of letters, several signed pledges in blood. I think we might have hit the golden mine with this. It appears that the former DCI wasn't quick enough in destroying all his material.'

Macleod had known it. He'd rushed. He'd rushed, and this find showed that to be the case.

'Good work, Jona. I'll get the team over. Start going through it. Can you get me photographs of it if you're not prepared to release the material yet?'

'I'll get it organised,' said Jona. 'Not a problem. Just get me a couple of your team to then sit and go through it.'

Macleod almost punched his fist in the air. Instead, he took a large gulp of coffee, chewed on it for a moment, and then it disappeared down his throat in the most satisfactory fashion. The phone rang again.

'This is Ross, sir. I've got the geeks, as you like to call them, working on the equipment. I don't know what else I can do here.'

'Get yourself over to Lawson's house', said Macleod.

'Lawson's house?'

'Yes,' said Macleod. 'Get over there. Jona has found a lot of material, letters, pledges signed in blood. We need to go through them. I want you and Clarissa on that.'

'Okay,' said Ross. 'Do we know if it's of any use?'

'No, I don't. Just get over and get on with it.'

'Okay. Sorry, sir,' said Ross.

He hadn't been meaning to be so questioning, but Macleod knew it was the wariness in Ross that brought about that comment. Clarissa would be happier though. She preferred more analogue things. Besides, he wanted her reading these letters because she probably understood more about occult matters than any of them. Certainly, Macleod was no expert. Clarissa would know when to note anything to Abby. He hoped that a location might come up, maybe the names of other members of the group.

His eyes crossed to the TV that was on in the far corner of his office. He grimaced when he saw his own face, but it was from a much older investigation, and had a caption at the bottom, *Macleod under pressure*. As if he didn't know that. The mural had been shown as well, every news outlet running it. That was the problem. You couldn't suppress something once somebody put it out. Now everyone was asking when were these things going to happen.

Well, Macleod knew when it was going to happen. A couple of days. That's what they'd said. That's what Abby had told him. He turned and looked out of the window and caught the outside of the station. Beyond the perimeter were a number of vans with satellite dishes on top. *No, that's not what we want. Every time I disappear out somewhere, they'll have a camera on me. Where's Macleod going? Is the case going to be solved?'*

He hated the press. Whenever he was the one to blame, they were all over him. Now he was the saviour. The press were people who could change their minds in an instant, only there to sell a story. What really bothered him was that people read this stuff as if it was automatically the truth. Usually, there was a lot of opinion, downright bad reporting, and a lack of nuance about people's circumstances that came into it.

Still, it wasn't something that was going away. At least Jim was taking care of it. He had a lot of admiration for the Assistant Chief Constable. He hadn't come back grovelling to Macleod, but instead, he'd been very matter of fact and simply got on with the job. This could, of course, have been the fact that it wasn't Jim's mistake to begin with, though Macleod thought he could have jumped in earlier. After all, he knew Macleod.

Lawson played it well. You had to give him that. Everyone thought he was just a dummy. He was anything but.

Macleod reached out for his coffee before then looking

151

back out of his window and he saw Jim had approached the press. There was a small circle forming around him, gradually getting bigger, recorders stuck in front of the man's face as he made a statement. The press would've seen the activity around Mr Patel's and Jim was there to keep them off it, just steer them into what should be reported. At last, we're getting someone to manage the press well instead of the deliberate mismanagement Lawson had done.

The phone ringing again, Macleod turned around and picked it up. 'Detective Inspector Seoras Macleod.'

'It's Hope,' said the voice from the other end. 'Sorry, Seoras. Dead end. We got to the house. There's been nobody in it for months, looks like it was just a pickup point, an address somebody checked. The house is pretty derelict. The only thing we found were a couple of rats.'

'Okay,' said Macleod. 'Jona has come up with something. A lot of correspondence and signed pledges in blood, hidden away in the walls of Lawson's house. Told Ross and Clarissa to get over there. You should probably join them.'

'Do you want me to stand down the firearms unit then?'

'There's not much for them to do now. Tell them to go back to their station, but to sit and wait, in case we dig anything up.'

It wasn't normal to have the firearms unit with them. Instead, they'd been assembled specifically because of the risk Macleod thought there was in approaching any new situation. He remembered being under the water with Clarissa, remembered how close it had been to them being dispatched. He certainly didn't want to go through that again. Every member of this team had been put at severe risk.

Macleod, having replaced the phone, wondered what to do next. He could sit and go through the old reports. Maybe he could get himself back over to Lawson's house. He was bothered by that because he knew he wouldn't sit and go through each and every bit of correspondence. They could do that. He'd need to take on board whatever was found. He needed to see the big picture.

Macleod was having a problem in the fact that this time, he wasn't able to simply decode everything. Lots of what was being written down came from languages that he had no idea about. The fact was, very few people did. Commonality amongst all of these killers, the commonality of Dark Union, was the fact that everybody in it could study to some degree, could look at such things as demonic language. Even if they were from the medieval ages and not highly thought of, they could study to know them, to understand the codes being put out. Macleod had already called these people 'true believers,' and his view hadn't diminished in the slightest.

He decided he would take a walk down to the canteen, grab himself some food as quickly as he could before coming back up to the office. As he stepped out into the corridors of the station, his mobile rang and he found Jane on the other end.'

'Do you need any new shirts?'

'What?' asked Macleod. 'What do you mean, do I need new shirts?'

'You've been on the telly. You're on the telly all the time. Papers and telly. Everything is about this case.'

'That's old footage of me.'

'Is it?' said Jane. 'I wondered because I thought I should get you some more shirts today. Maybe your other set of trousers and jacket.'

'Jim's taking the press. Jim's doing everything on the press, which is why it's all old footage,' said Macleod. 'I'm fine. I think we're nearly there on this. More like we're nearly at the end of the road. Not that we're stopping whatever's happening from happening.'

Jane could read him well. Even when he tried to be straight with her, the nuance of his worry came through.' 'Seoras, just believe, just keep going. You know you're in this situation for a reason. You know there's a reason why it's you.'

'That's very affirming,' he said. 'Right now, I'm not sure what's going to happen.'

'We never do, Seoras. Look, love, just try and relax, try and think. What are you going to do now?'

'Get something to eat,' said Macleod.

'Good,' said Jane. 'You think best when you're eating.'

'Do I?'

'Yes, you do. No distractions, going off to that place where that brain of yours works things out. Still don't know how you manage to do that. My brain just floods.'

'Well, the emptier it is, the easier it is to not get distracted,' said Macleod.

'Don't knock yourself, Seoras. I can do that happily. At the moment, trust yourself. Things will come. They always do.' Macleod answered in the affirmative, but he knew that was a lie. Things didn't always come. Sometimes he didn't get there. Sometimes the best you could do was mop it up afterwards and arrest the right people.

He had put out a word to the rest of the force, to report any missing children. So far, none had been taken. Maybe that was because it was a couple of days until the big event. Holding children for a time might be awkward, better to grab them nearer the time. It would give the police less time to follow up and possibly get clues.

154

Who was this broken-nose man? Where was Forbes and Whitelaw? For all the hunting and talk of these knives, he was yet to see one.

Macleod arrived at the short buffet at the heart of the station's canteen. The woman opposite placed a bit of steak pie on his plate when asked, followed by some roast potatoes and some sprouts. Apple juice went onto the tray as well. As he was about to slide it to the end to pay her, he noticed she was looking at him intently.

'Did I miss the gravy or something?' he asked.

'You go get them,' the woman said. 'We know you'll get them.'

Macleod gave a wry smile and whispered, 'Thank you.'

This was the problem with the TV. He'd be built up. *Here comes the hero.* He didn't feel like a hero. He felt like a man mucking out a stable in an attempt to find a wedding ring. He was doing everything he could do but all he needed right now was to sit down and have some food. Taking his tray, he made his way to a table in the middle of the cafeteria, sat down, and began to put the chewy crust of the steak pie into his mouth. It wasn't the best, but it would do. After all, the food was hot, warming. Outside was not. He heard a voice behind him.

'Inspector. Inspector.'

He turned and he saw the man who had punched him when he released Ian Lamb. One of his colleagues who had accused him of being derelict in what he had done and accused him with a punch.

'I'm glad you're on the case, sir.'

Macleod stood up, walked quickly over to the man, crouched down so he was at the same level as the man's face.

'I don't care what you think,' said Macleod. 'I don't know if we'll get this lot, but the one thing I'm not, is negligent. Next time you can just sort your facts out, son, before you start delivering justice.'

He returned back to the steak pie, aware of the silence around the room. It took him five minutes to polish off the food, and when he stood up, he knew that those around him were either in awe or in fear. Either would work for him. Either way, he was back. To cement that authority, he knew he'd need to get to solve this case on time.

Chapter 20

The day had been a long one when Macleod looked out of his office at the large team that currently occupied the main office beyond his own. Usually, he may have seen five, six, seven heads at most—a small team and a couple of assistants, but now, tables had been moved and in the middle was a large collection of letters. They weren't letters in truth. They were photocopies, for the real letters were with Jona, her team trying to match fingerprints and any DNA they could from them in an attempt to produce a name.

Macleod had sat back, letting his team get on with it. The previous hunt had ended in nothing at Bonar Bridge and the clock was now counting down. They were well into the night, but no one had gone home, all wishing to stay, do what they could and for that Macleod was immensely proud of them. He saw young constables who didn't need to impress him, but impressed he was by the dedication shown.

However, inside, he could feel his stomach beginning to knot. A day was gone. Tomorrow, sometime tomorrow. The notice of a day had been awkward. Would it happen at the start of the day? Would it be at midnight? There was no indication. However, if this had to be held in a public place you weren't going to do it at half-nine in the morning. You were going to do it during the darker hours, so Macleod hoped that they still had time.

He watched Ross marching between the different constables, encouraging them in that incredibly positive way he had. He never demeaned them. He was never over the top, always spurring them on. He had an ability to correct someone without them feeling like they were being chastised and yet he could see the strain on his face.

Ross's stomach was probably in the same position as Macleod's, but at least Ross was doing. Of course, Macleod was doing as well, thinking through everything that had happened, trying to get an idea of where to go, how to go, but he was coming up empty. Hope was out there amongst them. Ross was the one organising, so Hope, rather than stand back and pretend she was something, had dived in tearing through the letters as her red ponytail bobbed about. She grabbed paper after paper, scanning them, reading them, making notes, then going round the others and checking their notes to see if there was anything to be made from these letters.

Clarissa was sitting off somewhat. They'd found several pictures amongst the letters and she was sitting with them in front of her, studying the copies as if something magical would come to her. As was her custom, it being close to the middle of the night, she had a shawl on in the office, as she didn't trust the heating. *More like just getting old*, thought Macleod because he was feeling the cool of the office. He would turn the heat up, but the young ones would complain, and he needed them at their best.

Macleod stepped out of his office and saw several heads flick round towards him. He marched directly towards Hope, put a hand on her shoulder, bent down, and looked over, seeing her holding one of the parchments that had been signed in blood.

'They don't have names, do they?'

'That would be too easy, Seoras,' said Hope. 'Way too easy. According to Clarissa, these are demonic names. Names they give themselves.'

'Have we looked through computers? Got your geeks onto tracing these?'

'Done,' said Ross. 'I'm on it.' Macleod saw the man ready to deliver a tirade as if he was being accused of sloppy work, but then he stopped.

Macleod stood up, 'Good. Keep going.' He said to them all, 'Keep going. I'm proud of you.'

A few people stopped and looked at him, and for a moment it felt very uncomfortable, but then he saw some smiles, before a lot of the younger ones put their head back down and got on with their work.

'Shall I do the coffees?' suggested Macleod.

'I'll get them, sir; it's not a problem. Sit down. I'll bring it through for you.'

'Ross,' said Macleod. 'You're up to your eyeballs. Just get on. I'll do the coffee and when you've got something, bring it to me.' Macleod strode over to the coffee machine, emptied what was in before, and began grinding beans for another batch. By the time he had felt the machine making that gurgling noise as it boiled the water through, Hope appeared beside him. She lent in close.

'Wow,' she said, 'Mr Motivator today.'

'Going into the final day,' said Macleod. 'I had to do something. I've got nothing to think through. I've gone over everything and I can't find anything. This is us, seven kids with their lives on the line, and this is us.'

'We haven't got seven kids missing,' said Hope. 'The other departments are aware. They've reported nothing. Nobody knows anyone's missing.'

'Nobody knew Lawson's kid was missing either.'

'You didn't have to tell me that,' said Hope. 'I knew that. I was just saying positive.'

'I know, and that's why I told them, but you, me, Ross, Clarissa, we know it's looking bleak. Either we get lucky when they grab these kids and we can go after them, or we find something in this stuff. I don't think the man with the bust-up nose is going to appear. I don't think Forbes or Whitelaw are going to surface, not until the deed needs to be done. Yes. Jona comes over here or Abby comes up with something from that mural, or we get lucky with the kids, and honestly, I'd say our chances are ten percent at best. Then the backlash will begin.'

'Chin up.' said Hope. 'We're not dead in the water yet.'

'No,' said Macleod and as he turned, so he faced the group again, he gave a smile. 'Who's milk?' he said. 'Although milk, of course, is wrong in a coffee.' He saw a few of them laugh. A few hands went up, and it took him the next five minutes to pass out the coffees, getting several of them wrong. He popped one down in front of Clarissa.

'How's it going?' he asked.

'Shush,' she said. Macleod watched as she stared at four different pictures.

'What are these from?'

'From his house, shush.' Macleod stepped back over to the coffee machine where Hope was standing, drinking her coffee.

'What's up with her?'

'Just thinking,' said Hope. 'It didn't take a detective to work that out.'

'Wouldn't speak to me. Wouldn't even tell me what she was doing.'

'Well, sometimes you let people do their job.' Macleod shot Hope a look. 'She's different,' said Hope. 'Clarissa is different, works differently, sees things differently. That mural, the old books and that, it's her field. Let her operate on this. Let her be her.'

'Okay,' said Macleod. 'I'll just go over then.'

'No,' said Hope, 'Don't. You just want something you can put your teeth into. You just want something you can work on. It's not here yet. Just leave it.'

Hope stopped speaking as they watched Clarissa stand up, take two of the pictures, and suddenly march out of the office. The rest of the team stopped momentarily, staring at the now swinging door before putting their heads back down and continuing their work.

'Anyone, any idea?' asked Macleod suddenly. 'Anyone know where she's going?'

There was silence. He turned back to Hope, leaning in and saying quietly, 'Just let Clarissa be Clarissa. Just let her get on with it. Is she having a breakdown or has she found something?'

'Who knows? I wouldn't get in the way of a Rottweiler though,' said Hope and gave Macleod a grin. 'She's onto something. She'll tell you when she's ready. This must be eating you up, not having something to do, not having . . .'

'That's enough, Sergeant,' said Macleod quietly. 'I'll be in my office if you need me. You can tell me when the coffee's all done.'

Macleod walked back to his office and in truth, his heart was pounding. What was it Clarissa had seen? He wanted to run down after her, jump in a car wherever she was going and just be there but instead he was stuck in the office waiting. With his own coffee in hand, he did what he usually did and turned to the window at the rear of his office looking out at the lights of Inverness.

Seven kids, he thought. *They're going to grab seven kids. Where? From where? From a home, from a hospital? What? Would they be babies or smaller children? Most so far have been toddlers and up. Innocence. Total innocence.*

He could feel his hands gripping tight, a sense of rage flowing through him. He remembered Gleary, taking out his anger on his niece. He remembered the fact that she was not left intact. He felt like doing that to the people committing these crimes against the children. Part of him felt like ripping them apart. It's what they deserved, wasn't it? He was struggling at this moment to see redemption, to see a second chance for people like this. They were more than cold-blooded murderers. They were actually doing this out of worship. Doing this because . . . well, he never fully understood that side, did he?

There was a knock at the door, and it was pushed open.

'Seoras,' said Hope. 'Come here.'

He spun and almost ran around the desk, following Hope to the big table in the middle of the office. Ross was pointing at a couple of letters sitting amidst the pile.

'This demon signed Andulin. Andulin's mentioned here in this letter, this letter over here. My team of techs have found the name on the dark web. They've traced Andulin back to an account and that through to an address. However, the address changes over time and we're not sure that Andulin doesn't actually change either because look at the handwriting

where it's signed in blood, and it's signed
Andulins but the signature's not the sam

the

'But you have addresses,' said Macleod

'Ones up in Tain,' said Hope, 'and th
maville.'

'Jemimaville? On the Black Isle? He knew it. It was at the
far end of the Black Isle. He'd driven through the little village
with Jane several times. She liked making a circuit of it, going
from one side of the Black Isle along one coast and round to
the other. Jemimaville had a bird-watching station right at the
end of the village. He said village but it wasn't really that big.
A collection of houses, an old garage at the end, and there was
somebody like this amongst that, that almost idyllic look?

'Get a team,' said Macleod, 'and go to Tain.'

Hope nodded.

'I'll wake up the firearm squad. Probably take them about
an hour to get here and ready to go.'

'No,' said Macleod. 'We're beyond midnight. We're in the
day. We go.'

Hope nodded, turned around, and shouted at a couple of the
constables.

'Grab some from down below if you can,' said Macleod. 'Be
careful, but don't wait.'

'And you?' asked Hope.

'I'm off to Jemimaville with,' he pointed, 'you, you, you, and
you.'

'No,' said Ross, 'Don't. Don't take Anderson. Leave, leave
Margo as well.'

'Just give me some people then,' said Macleod. 'And whoever
it is, outside in two minutes, the back door.'

He turned and marched off, hearing Ross begin to organise

people behind him.

'And you stay here, Ross,' he said over the top of his shoulder. 'Keep going in case these leads are duds.'

'Of course,' said Ross.

'And find out where Clarissa is,' he said. 'Update her on what's going on. Use that as the excuse just in case it ties in with whatever she's been spotting.'

He marched through the door of his own office, grabbed his coat and a hat, and made for the back car park of the station. As his feet trundled down the stairs, he could feel his heart pounding. He was back on it. This was the hunt! He only hoped he was in time.

Chapter 21

The little green sports car sped towards Aviemore, a cold wind racing across Clarissa's face. She kept the top down to keep her awake as she drove, but in truth, her pounding heart was probably enough. She only expected to see pictures. At first, looking at them, she hadn't thought they were portraits that could mean anything, but then Ross had put them in front of her and something in her brain had said, 'I know these. I know where these are from.'

Two of the images were rather grotesque, creatures that certainly didn't exist in real life. One had a fiery lake of sulphur, and the last picture, the last picture Macleod would have reviled at if he'd realised who the central figure was. She couldn't remember the name of it. What was the name of the picture? Where had she seen it? It had been somewhere, somewhere important. Somewhere . . .

Oh, it was too much. She'd been young, back in the day, when she'd been able to command attention. Those wonderful days when you're in your youth. When men would look at you and you could wrap them around your little finger without having to pummel them with your fists at the same time. You didn't have to be cunning. You didn't have to be able to play it cool, be able to work them. They were like lap dogs.

Still, she thought, those days were long gone. Where had she been in those days? It started out with art as a hobby. She'd gone on to the beat as a young officer, a young officer who had been described as spunky by her sergeant. She'd taken all the compliments and leery comments that came her way, had wowed them with apparent ease, and excelled as an officer. She never really truly got her just desserts from that. Some men had got in the way; some who were right idiots.

Maybe now was easier; maybe it wasn't. Maybe it was still as hard for the young women starting out. She didn't know as she wasn't a young woman anymore. At the time, her hobby had been art and she had travelled. She travelled up and down in that little number she had, the sports car of its day and she'd been somewhere. Been somewhere to an exhibition. That's where she'd seen it.

First, it was en route to Abby because Abby might know where things were now. She pulled the car up in front of the flat and rang the buzzer. There was no answer. She rang it again and kept her finger on it until Abby responded.

'What on earth? It's like . . . is it three in the morning?'

'Let me up', said Clarissa. 'I've got something, you need to see this.'

'Right now?'

'We're past our time on this,' said Clarissa sharply. 'This could be enacted; it could be happening now. I have no time. Open the damn door and I'll come up.'

When the buzzer went, Clarissa pushed the door with force, stomped up the stairs ignoring the fact that she was clumping loudly, albeit with a bit of a stutter, until she reached the door of the flat. Abby pulled it open and Clarissa marched in. She turned to the woman handing over the pictures she'd brought from the office.

'What are these?' asked Abby. Clarissa realised that the woman was in a long T-shirt and not much else. Abby caught her look. 'I've just got out of bed.' She took the pictures, slapped them down on the coffee table and sat on the sofa looking at them. 'What do you want me to do with these?' she asked.

'I've seen these somewhere,' said Clarissa. 'I've seen them. It's a long time ago, a very long time ago. That one on the end.'

'It's the Damnation of Christ,' said Abby. 'That was outlawed, put away for a while, but I'm sure it was picked up again. Back then, it was big news. It was . . . well, I say big news, but it was certainly important in the art world.'

'Yes. I went to see it. I went to see the collection,' said Clarissa, 'I went to . . .' She turned around and saw a man standing in his boxer shorts looking at her from a bedroom door.

'Sorry, Mike. This is work. Mike, Clarissa.'

Clarissa looked at Mike and reckoned that Abby had a similar taste in men to herself back in the day when she was first looking for this picture. Mike might have been the man she would've caught hold of as well.

'Do you know where to make coffee, Mike?' said Clarissa, suddenly.

Mike simply nodded.

'Be a dear then, Mike,' said Abby. 'I don't know how long this will take. Get us both a coffee. Make yourself one too as well if you want.'

'I'll just go and put something on,' said Mike.

He didn't have to, thought Clarissa, and then she shook her

167

head. She needed to get focused. She plonked herself down beside Abby.

'That one,' said Abby, 'The Damnation of Christ. It's been about. It wasn't something they wanted on the black market. It was something that was picked up,' she said. 'Fifteen years ago, who picked it up?'

'What do you mean they didn't want it on show?' asked Clarissa.

'Certain items are stored away by the big libraries. Trusted to them for safekeeping, historically valuable, but things that they consider to be potentially dangerous. Things that could stir people into actions you don't want them to be involved in. They go to special collections, collections that are held away.'

'They're just books, aren't they?'

'Indeed, they are, but we've got people about to commit the murder of seven children and five previously because they believe their master will come back to this world in a big way and cause pestilence over the land. Are the books and images and things truly dangerous in their own right?' said Abby. 'Probably not.'

'What do you mean, probably?' asked Clarissa. 'They're not dangerous, are they? They . . . they're just books and words.'

'Well, that's what we'd like to hope but I take nothing for granted. Either way, it doesn't matter. We need to find this.'

'Why?' asked Clarissa. 'It was amongst a collection of letters. It's probably just some artwork, isn't it?'

'No,' said Abby. 'These guys have been on a trail. You don't just know what to do with these knives, or how to dispatch all these children. They're following a particular time and destination to do it. They're following a specific method. That mural being put up said so much but they've got that from somewhere. The images within it were reaching beyond what I know here,' said Abby. 'I think there's a book somewhere more detailed. We've had pages explaining things but maybe the original is somewhere.'

'Wouldn't somebody have brought it forward?'

'How?' asked Abby. 'The murals on the wall, you've got just a mural. The signs and symbology, would you bring them out? If you think what this actually is and if you honestly believe in it, there's no way you'd bring it up to the surface. On the other hand, people might think it's a crackpot's thing and it's hidden away now, stored, not thought about. Not every museum has a curator who is older than the books inside it. Not all curators understand every item they have.'

Abby jumped up. Clarissa watched her swagger, making her way over to her laptop bag, hauling out the flat black device and then flipping it open and putting it on the coffee table.

'Let's find out where it is. This picture at least.'

'Where do you think I saw it?' asked Clarissa.

'I don't know,' said Abby. 'You'll need to try and tell me. It could be a lot quicker.'

'Let me think,' she said. 'I was attending an exhibition.'

'Where? What part of the country were you in?' asked Abby.

'Driven down to London,' said Clarissa. 'London. That's where it was. It was Reinhardt,' said Clarissa.

'Who's Reinhardt?' asked Abby.

'Reinhardt had the best backside you've ever seen.'

Abby looked at her. 'I kind of need to know more than that. This computer doesn't have a database of fine-looking bottoms.'

'He really did though,' said Clarissa. 'He was also to do with Freiburg. He had collections in Freiburg.'

'Now we're running,' said Abby. Clarissa watched her delve into the screen tapping away on the keyboard. 'Reinhardt Freiburg,' she said. 'Got it. Possibly got a list of collections here. Do you read German?' asked Abby.

'No.'

'Damn . . . Mike, how's your German?' shouted Abby, over her shoulder.

'Gut,' he said laughing.

'Sit down here, hun. Have a look at this.'

Mike marched over and Abby looked at Clarissa. 'Get up and finish the coffee,' she said. 'Mike, read that for me.'

Clarissa went over to make the coffee and heard the couple conversing. Mike was translating newspaper articles in front of him and Abby was specifying different parts of it to be translated.

'Special collection,' heard Clarissa. 'Given away deemed not palatable or interesting for the daily general public.'

'That's it,' said Abby. 'That's it. Where did that go? Where did that go?'

'The British Museum,' said Mike. 'That says it's going to the British Museum.'

'We need to check there,' said Abby. 'We need to check the collections.'

'Can't you get it online?'

'This is not going to be listed,' said Abby. 'Don't you get what I've been talking about? Since you've gone and seen this, it's gone back underground. It's got put away. He's actually realised, Reinhardt, what the point of this is, that this is dangerous.'

'We need to go to the British Museum. Wake them up, get into their vaults. Is that what you're saying?' asked Clarissa.

'Exactly,' said Abby.

'Grab a bag then. Get some clothes on.'

'Sorry, Mike,' said Clarissa. 'You're going to have to hold fort here.' Clarissa saw Abby stand up and watched poor Mike's eyes as he trailed her into the bedroom. Clarissa picked up her phone and dialled Macleod's office number.

'This is Ross. I'm trying to get hold of you. Boss wants to know what you're doing.'

'Got a lead. Got to go down to London.'

'London?' queried Ross. 'We're on a deadline here. We haven't time to go to London.'

'Exactly.' She closed down the call almost immediately and dialled Macleod.

'Seoras,' she said. It sounded like he was in a car, racing along.

'Clarissa, what's up?'

Clarissa explained the situation and of the possible link. 'I'm chasing one here. Hope's away for one too. We've got possible addresses. How important is this?' He asked.

'These pictures match. They come from a collection that I saw when I was a lot younger. Abby thinks they've gone underground with it. Abby thinks they could be the source material that they've been using.'

'What does that mean?'

'You want to know when and where? This might tell us. We might be able to work it out from it.'

'Phone the Assistant Chief Constable. Tell Jim that I've okayed it. He needs to get you down to London ASAP. I don't care what you have to do,' said Macleod. 'If this is an opportunity and a chance, you raise merry hell and tell me what's in this collection that they are going for.'

'Will do,' said Clarissa. 'It's a long drive though.'

'Tell Jim it's his job to get you there ASAP. I don't want you taking ten or twelve hours getting down. I want you down there in the next couple of hours and in and looking.'

'That's not going to be easy, Seoras,' said Clarissa.

'You're my Rottweiler. You blooming well make it easy,' he said. 'We didn't all get half-killed to not get a flight and come up short.'

Clarissa put the phone down and began to look up the number for the Assistant Chief Constable. Part of her was shaking. She'd never gone to an Assistant Chief Constable before with information like this. Yes, there was trepidation, but there was also excitement. This was something and it was time to act. She pressed the numbers on her phone. 'Be a Rottweiler,' Seoras had said. Well, the bit was between her teeth.

Chapter 22

The last thing Clarissa had expected was to be flown down to the British museum. Granted, she wasn't exactly on a business jet, and she hadn't caught the first flight down, but instead was sitting up front in the company of Jim, the Assistant Chief Constable. She hadn't known he was a pilot with his own Beechcraft at Inverness Airport. Had Seoras known, or had he just struck lucky with what the Assistant Chief Constable was capable of?

It was certainly going to be quicker than using the car. Sitting behind her was Abby, who didn't look so excited to be on the plane. Maybe Abby was used to flying more plush aircraft. Clarissa wondered why. Yes, she was big in the line of artwork that she specialised in, but Clarissa never saw it as paying that much money. Or did she do other things on the quiet? After all, Abby had been a thief, one that Clarissa couldn't catch. Still, the important thing was the woman was here now and working with her and despite Mike's sad look as she left the flat, Abby was focused and seemed to share the same excitement that Clarissa had, that they might be getting somewhere.

Despite being able to fly, Jim had also been required to pull a few strings and he landed in the dawn at a small airfield just outside of the greater London area. As he parked the aircraft, a police car was waiting and the three of them were sped into the middle of London, direct to the British Museum. On arrival, they were escorted by one of the senior curators into an office to be offered coffee.

'We can't wait,' said Clarissa. 'This is important.'

'As I understand it,' said the curator, who seemed to be a similar age to Clarissa, 'we're quite unaware of what it is you're looking for. We got the message that it arrived here sometime in the past.'

'A German paper refers to it coming here,' said Abby. 'It contains certain pages from a manuscript referring to occult matters.' She pulled some of the pages and pictures that she had acquired regarding the whole incident. The curator shook his head.

'Do you have somewhere you keep special collections?' asked Abby, knowing fine rightly that he did. 'I mean the stuff that's not talked about, that I couldn't look up online. I've searched through your other library, and you don't have it in it. This would be the more private collection hidden away in the back.'

'We don't have something like that.'

Jim stepped forward. 'I'm the Assistant Chief Constable and this is an investigation of the most urgent seriousness. We've had many children die already. Anything that's revealed here will be kept quiet and will not be spread beyond the three of us, only what needs to be told in order for the investigation to continue. I don't think you would like it if I have to come in and search the British Museum separately. I wouldn't like it either. It would cause certain ruffles, shall we say? We need your help,' said Jim. 'Everything here will be treated as confidential.'

The man stepped back for a moment, regarded Clarissa and

Abby.

'You do know who this woman is? She's rumoured to have .
. .'

'I'm rumoured to have done a lot of things,' said Abby.

'What this woman is,' said Clarissa, 'is the best in this line of
work. Trust me, if she wasn't, I wouldn't have her near a mile
of here.' Abby glowered over Clarissa. 'But she's what I need
at the moment, and she's got to the bottom of this. Please, we
need to go and have a look in your other collection.'

'I'll hold you responsible if any of this gets out,' the curator
said to the Assistant Chief Constable.

'Of course, but let's get on, please. Time is of the essence.'

The man nodded, held up his hands, and took them back
out of the office and over to a lift that descended to the
bottom floors of the museum. It was still reasonably early
in the morning and the museum hadn't opened, but there were
staff milling about. Several of them watched as the curator
disappeared down different aisles.

There was a unique system where everything was stacked up
together in what looked like mobile shelves that then parted
so that they formed an aisle that you could walk down looking
at whatever it was on either side. When they came together, it
clearly saved a lot of space.

The curator didn't go to any filing system but merely kept
walking until he got to the end of the large vault and passed
into another room. Here, his retina was scanned. He put a
hand up so that his thumbprint was recognised before a door
opened and he led them into a room with a smaller but similar
filing system. He stepped along it, spun a handle and opened
up a particular aisle and then marched down it. He pointed
up to the right-hand side.

'Do you need a table? Everything relating to that sort of picture is up there.'

'A table would be great,' said Clarissa. The curator coughed for a moment before Abby distributed gloves.

Jim said, 'Abby, it'd probably be best if I don't touch anything. These things need to be handled correctly. Clarissa will know how.'

'Very carefully,' said the curator. He disappeared out of the aisle for a moment before coming back in and setting up a small table. There were no chairs, but Abby reached up and took several boxes down onto the table. She opened up the lid and started looking through it before boxing up again and placing it back up on the shelves. Eight boxes in, Abby pulled out a dusty tome and placed it on the table. There was writing on the front, in a language that Clarissa had no knowledge of.

'What's that?' asked Jim.

'It's hard to pronounce the title because it's in a language that we don't know how it was spoken. Basically, it's a pictography of everything we've been investigating. There's a story here, a story of how you summon something and what you have to do to make it occur.' She opened the book carefully as the curator drew breath, watching Abby's eyes flashing along it.

'Am I okay to take pictures?' asked Abby.

'You absolutely are not,' said the curator. 'You can look at it, but nothing leaves here. If you have to make notes for the investigation, then notes can be made, but no images. We don't want it known that it is here.'

'And do you trust Abby to do that?' asked Clarissa.

'No, he doesn't,' said Abby. 'He wouldn't be showing us this except for the murder investigation. This will be on the move. They don't have one vault like this. There are others. This will be placed in a different one, to make sure that I don't know where it is. It's probably a wise precaution.'

Abby smiled at the man. Clarissa realised that the young woman was incredibly engaging. The older curator, who was at first angry at her presence, seemed to suddenly be warming to her. It was a charm offensive, backed up by visual appeal. Clarissa remembered the day when she was capable of that. Nowadays she was more of a blunt hammer.

'Let's get on,' said Jim. 'See if you can find what you need.'

Abby stood looking through the book. She pointed at some of the pictures inside. 'Here,' she said. 'Here's the instruction for those that have died before. Innocents, waifs, strays. Those are widows, single mums, I guess nowadays. Those who can't support themselves, there,' she said, pointing to a page that was full of symbols.

'Jona said these symbols were from different places,' said Clarissa. 'These symbols are Mayan, there's Aztec, all over.'

'I never said this book was accurate,' said Abby. 'Understand, this is created in the Middle Ages. This is created out of histories of other religions. That's why the symbols are there. They've tied in that these other religions are somehow part and parcel of the anti-Christ movement. Frankly, I think it's nonsense, but we're not here to think what's nonsense. We're here to think like they think,' said Abby, 'and they think this is real, very real.' She focused back on the book again. 'Here,' she said. 'This is it. This tells you how to find the right slaughter site, ritual slaughter,' she said when Jim tutted. 'I'm not being gross. I'm just saying what is and also the time. If we know the time, then we can find the site.'

'Let's get on it,' said Clarissa. Abby sat down, and started writing notes down under the careful eye of the curator. When she started to write a second line, he stopped her. 'That's got nothing to do with the instructions,' he said.

'I didn't think you were the main curator. You're a specialist in this too.'

'Not to your level. I know who you are,' he said. 'More than aware of who you are. Keep it to what the police are trying to do.'

'And do it quick,' said Clarissa suddenly, frowning at the woman. She thought that Abby would've been all about the kids, but she wasn't, and yet Clarissa needed her.

'Okay, okay,' said Abby. Quickly, she started writing down many different notes. However, the curator seemed happy with what she was doing, and he was watching her so close. Clarissa was amazed at the man's patience. There was maybe two hours involved of making notes, referring backwards and forwards throughout the tome, and from other pages that Abby had with her.

'You know this isn't complete,' said Abby. 'Do you want a copy of the pages that are missing? I have them in my satchel. These will complete the book.'

'No,' said the curator. 'I think it's dangerous enough as it is.'

Clarissa wondered just what people thought of this type of literature. It seemed strange, but as far as she was concerned, there was nothing crazy about it. Everything was based around the fact that a load of nutters were going to commit ritual sacrifice. She didn't believe a word of it.

'I've got it,' said Abby. 'I've got it.'

'Where and when?' blurted Jim.

'The when we know,' said Clarissa. 'It's now. It's today.'

'Where?' asked Jim.

'As far as I can see from this map,' said Abby, holding her

phone out in front of her, 'it's a place called Loch Fannich, west of Inverness. That's probably why they're so concentrated around Inverness.'

'Why Inverness?' asked Jim.

'The Middle Ages, everything was about here. Everything was about the angel isle, the UK. You never heard Jerusalem. Some people actually thought Christ walked here.'

'I'll get upstairs, alert Macleod,' said Clarissa.

'Well, if we're done,' said the curator, 'I think we'll put everything away. We'll search you before you leave,' he said to Abby. Clarissa gave a smirk.

'You also.'

'I'm a police officer,' said Clarissa. She caught Abby's smile as the curator simply shook his head.

* * *

Macleod arrived at Jemimaville, entering the tiny village in a convoy of four cars, and they pulled up in front of a whitewashed house. The large brickwork was crumbling in parts, but there was a white door with black numbers on it and a large knocker. If Macleod looked up, he could see nothing inside. No movement inside, just lace curtains across the windows.

'What time of day is it?' he asked. 'Shouldn't people be getting up now?'

He rapped the door and as he did so, he found it swung open. Carefully, he stepped inside. 'With me,' he said to two of the constables. 'The rest of you, outside. Keep an eye. Somebody, get round the back.'

Macleod walked in and saw the damp patch where the door

had been left open, possibly through the night. He walked and turned right into a living room where yesterday's fire had died out in the grate. He looked over at the single large rocking chair that was opposite the television. Slumped across it was a man with grey hair. He may have been in his sixties, but he certainly wasn't going to age anymore. Macleod saw the slash across the throat and if that wasn't enough, the blood all over the clothing confirmed the man was certainly dead.

Chapter 23

Macleod heard the message from Clarissa, looked at the scene in front of him, instructed one of the constables to get more officers here, and then tore out of the house. As he ran for the car, his mobile phone went off again, and he saw Hope's face looking back at him from the lit screen. He pressed the button to accept the call.

'Seoras, I've just got the Tain, and . . .'

'Your suspect is dead. They've cleaned up. I know. Just had a message from Clarissa. Abby's found where it is, Loch Fannich. We need to head for Loch Fannich. I'm going to send everyone on ahead. Just meet us there as soon as you get the chance. Leave a small posse to protect your scene but get over there.'

'Understood,' said Hope. Macleod closed the call. He jumped into the passenger seat of his car. The young constable beside him tore away from the scene like his life depended on it.

As the car sped along, Macleod called the station, requesting that anyone near Loch Fannich should head there immediately where there was the possibility that there may be children in trouble.

The car drove along, passing through Culbokie, and then through Dingwall and Strathpeffer. Macleod began to think about the location. Loch Fannich was off the beaten track, not easy to get to. First, it was in a strange place to commit ritual sacrifice, but then again, how did you make sense of this? Why out there? Why here in Scotland? They were basing things off what they believe were ancient texts, but if he remembered what Abby said, the book was written in the Middle Ages, Medieval times.

As far as his history took him, and that wasn't that far, they were times of great superstition, but also of forms of Christianity spreading throughout the land, although quite how evolved they were, he wasn't too sure. Maybe he was just occupying his mind racing to the scene. His phone went again, and he picked it up, realising it was the station calling. The sergeant on duty was Sergeant Ingram.

'Seoras, they've picked up seven kids from a playgroup. Barged in with weapons and stole them away. Took them by name. As far as we can gather, they are all single mothers' kids.'

We aren't too late then, thought Macleod. They could still get to the scene. There was still time. He turned to his driver, urging him to go faster.

It all made sense. It tidied up the loose ends. They would go out now, and they would commit this mass murder, this sacrifice. They were going to do it in the daylight. Well, either that or they would do it tonight. Maybe they would arrive on scene with everyone there. Either way, they could scupper their plans.

Macleod phoned the same station back, advising the sergeant to get all stations looking, keeping seven young children under wraps wouldn't be easy. It took Macleod over half an hour to get there. When he did, he had to trudge in his good shoes across moorland, down to the edge of Loch Fannich. A small contingent had beat him to it, and Hope arrived soon afterwards. They set up road stops, to make sure nobody could get close. Macleod looked around. It was just a loch. There was nowhere, nowhere for the scene. Where would you stand? Where would you go? It struck him as odd, but at least they were here now. Here.

The rest of the daylight hours passed slowly as a large police presence remained. Macleod didn't want to leave, not in case the children turned up and he may have to bargain his way out with their lives. An armed contingent was there as well, hidden away, but ready to move in a moment's notice. Cars were stopped approaching, but no one had young children that either didn't belong to them or didn't fit the description of those who were taken. Macleod had everything. Photographs, details about their parents and officers asked kids directly who they belonged to, who was looking after them. Other parents were asked to prove who was in the back seat of the car, but all checked out.

As the day wore on towards night, Macleod began to get nervous. They hadn't come. They weren't here. By late evening, the press had had the story. It was on the news where they were and Macleod thought that the likelihood of carrying out the killing would be small. Clarissa had arrived back up from London, flown back by Jim, and had sent Abby back off home. As they retreated back to the station that night, close to nine, Macleod thought they'd missed the opportunity, and he needed to get a round table to work out what would happen next. Was there a secondary option? Was there something these people would do that would negate the killing? Was there some way in which they could still make this forced ritual happen?

As he sat in his office, he could see the dejected faces outside. Clarissa was on the phone, checking through what had happened, making sure that they'd had the right place, but everything had seemed correct. She had talked to Abby several times through the day.

The door opened and Ross filed through, looking dejected.

'They've still got them,' he said to Macleod. 'They're still holding them, sir. I thought if we'd discovered their plans, they'd just let them go.'

'Wishful thinking, Ross. These people, they're not rational. This is all about pleasing their master. I said before, true believers. They're the worst kind. They do without thinking.'

'I thought that's what you were meant to be. Obedient. That's what Christians are, aren't they?'

'Not blind, not just wandering about not challenging what they're looking at. So, no, Ross. We're not meant to be, at least not as I see it.' Macleod reckoned he was drifting because Ross wasn't really listening. Instead, Ross went through the mechanical motion of taking out papers from a file, reading them through before he would talk at the round table. Macleod shrugged. Ross hadn't brought any coffee through. Clarissa hobbled into the room, still looking in pain.

'Bought some time, Seoras. I think we've bought some time.'

'I wish I was that confident,' said Macleod. 'I'm not sure.'

'It wasn't easy you know. It wasn't easy for Abby. A lot of variables when you're doing that thing. You think you know what words are? Languages are not simple. You were breaking a code. They'd use symbols but they weren't using them in their actual meanings. This was written in that crazy language. I'm amazed at how well she knew it. She is into that thing.

The curator was not happy with her being there. Jim basically put an instruction to him.'

Macleod was only half listening, his mind churning through what could be going on.

'I don't think we'll see Jona tonight. She's still tidying up. We left her with a lot of crime scenes. The two individuals we're still looking at identifying because they're not who they say they were. Their names were of people that died a long time ago. They changed their identity, so unlike the others, they knew how to hide in plain sight.'

'They didn't know how to hide from their own though,' said Macleod. 'Once the address is right, they just finished them. Forbes or whoever else.'

Macleod looked off into the distance. In the far corner of the room, he saw a spider climbing down the wall. It wasn't particularly large, and his eyes fixed on it just as somewhere to stare, not to have to look at the dejected faces of his colleagues.

'The thing is,' Clarissa continued, 'it was a difficult translation at one point, Abby almost confused seven waifs for seven heads. Can you imagine it? Because if we'd got that wrong, we wouldn't have got to Loch Fannich. We wouldn't have managed to be in the right place. It's a good job she did. It was funny because there was two ways of looking at it, but the older manuscript, it went back to say that you were looking for waifs, not heads. Then on the map that led us to Loch Fannich. It's a good job she called it, or it might have been over by now.'

'Hang on,' said Macleod, suddenly, his eyes fixed on Clarissa. 'You said that the older manuscript, the older bit was what you were working off. What do you mean?'

'The language itself, you try to work out what it means, and you can only do that, because you don't know the language, by going off other manuscripts that that maybe have translations from further back. Therefore, you work out what the language means. Now, the older ones are probably more accurate; therefore, you go with them and that's why we got waifs and not heads. Like I said, it would've put us in a completely different position.'

'But this was worked out in medieval times. These manuscripts you talk about to work out the language, are they older?'

'Yes,' she said. 'You have to go back to the really old ones to get the true understanding, not the . . .'

'Stop!' said Macleod. 'But if you're in the middle ages, which one are you working off?'

Clarissa stared back at him. 'Well, you might not be able to get hold of older ones. It might have been the . . .'

'Get hold of Abby,' he said. 'Work it out using heads, not waifs.' Clarissa grabbed her phone, tried to stand up, but found herself shaking as she dialled the number.

'Hope, get everybody ready. We're on the move,' shouted Macleod.

'Where to?'

'We'll know when Abby works it out, but get the teams, all of them.'

'Well, most of them are up at Loch Fannich.'

'Tell them to get ready to move. Only split them,' said Macleod. 'In case we get this wrong, keep half of them there. The other half on the move.'

Macleod followed Clarissa out to the main office where she was still on the phone to Abby. 'On speaker phone,' said Macleod. Clarissa glared at him but put the phone down and pressed for the speaker to activate.

'I'm not sure why I'm doing this,' said Abby.

'Entertain me,' said Macleod suddenly.

'Inspector?' she said.

'Entertain me. I think you might have made a mistake using the older translations. I think the people who wrote this might have been in a later version.'

'You could be right, Inspector,' said Abby. 'You could be right, but that would totally change . . .'

'I know. Follow it through. Get me a location, now.' There was silence on the other end of the phone, and then Macleod could hear people moving. He was standing for five minutes.

'The well of the seven heads, that's a marker. Based on that, and moving the distance away from it, further down and the other locations that are mentioned,. . . I'd say we're looking at . . . Loch Garry.'

'Are you certain?' asked Macleod.

'As much as I can be.'

Macleod turned on his heel. 'Ross, Clarissa, Hope, Loch Garry, now.'

The team sprinted for the door, running down to the car park. Macleod looked at his watch. Half past nine. It was dark all around. Would they be too late? He grabbed a constable as he ran out into the car park.

'Tell the duty sergeant to round up whoever he can. Loch Garry, now. If he asks why, tell him Inspector Macleod wants that detail.'

Macleod could see the Assistant Chief Constable walking in from the car park. 'What's up, Seoras?' he said, seeing Macleod sprint past him.

'We got the wrong location,' Macleod shouted. 'We got the wrong location. We can still stop it.'

Macleod didn't wait for the Assistant Chief Constable to ask any further questions or even to join him. Instead, he was in the car, along with Hope, and they tore out of the police station. Loch Garry was south, a reasonable distance south as well. Hope put the foot down, racing out of Inverness. Macleod hoped they were right. He hoped they had got this. There had to be time. There had to be time. He looked at his watch again: two hours. Two hours and maybe twenty-five minutes of today left. He had to be on time. As he sped along, he found himself praying as hard as he'd ever had in his life.

Chapter 24

The road out to Loch Garry swept past Macleod in different shades with darkness. Between the odd streetlight, he could see a tree here or there, but the night was dark, clouds covering the sky and no stars to be seen. Outside, it was fiercely cold and the only light inside the car was that of the instrument panel in front of Hope. The air conditioning was droning on, keeping Macleod warm on the road out to Loch Garry. He was on his second set of shoes for the day, for when he arrived at Loch Fannich, he'd found that they'd got soaked traipsing over the moorland.

The armed response team were on their way, having raced down from Loch Fannich and Macleod thought they might just reach the new location ahead of the team. It was on the northern side of the loch as indicated on the map. Macleod wondered whether or not it had been Abby that had got her translations wrong, or whether or not it had been Forbes and his people. He didn't know. He just knew that Loch Fannich had attracted no satanic worship.

The car swept across the northern side of Loch Garry, looking down towards the water that was in darkness. The armed response team and several constables had raced on ahead, lights blaring, but they hadn't reported finding anything on this side of the loch. It was significant in size and Macleod heard through the radio that nothing unusual had been seen up the north side.

'Looks like another blowout, Seoras,' said Hope. 'Maybe they'd seen us at Fannich and just didn't bother. Maybe they were a little bit smarter, decided to call it off, but I don't know where they've put the kids.'

Macleod stared, looking for the water in the dark that was ahead. 'Let's not be so sure,' looking at his watch. The hour was past ten. 'It's perfect,' he said, 'perfect for what they want to do.' He glanced to the far side of the loch. 'Let's take a spin round there. Think about it,' he said to Hope. 'If we, or they, managed to screw up the instructions for Fannich, who knows how accurate they are getting to here. They might be out. They might have . . .'

'Okay,' said Hope. 'We'll do it. We'll cover the whole loch. It can't hurt. The north side's protected, anyway.'

Hope reversed the car, and after turning it around, drove round to the south side of Loch Garry. The road was a reasonable distance from the edge, but there were a few spots where tracks led up towards the water.

Macleod thought he saw a light, then there was nothing. Hope's beam lit up the road ahead until she saw a couple of cars. They were parked, but there was a minibus further ahead. Macleod jumped out of the car, took his flashlight, and started peering into the rear of one of the cars where he saw a white cloth and thought he could hear something in the distance. There was a reasonable breeze blowing, so it wasn't easy to pick out the noises from those he would associate with night time. Instead, everything sounded muffled.

'I think we should call the teams over here,' said Macleod to Hope, still in the car. 'I really think we should.' His torch scanned the front of him, and he saw a small track. On the wind he could hear a chant. 'This way,' he said to Hope, 'get them down here.'

Macleod tore off as quick as he could down the path. The further he went, the louder he could hear the chant. It was low level at the moment, but as he ran closer, he could make out several shapes in the dark. As Macleod got nearer, the shapes in the darkness changed into figures and the chanting began to rise. He could see a small group held off to one side, while in the middle of a circle chanting was in full flow, knives held up to the sky.

He swept the pen torch ahead of him and caught the sight of a child in the beam before he heard Hope behind him.

'How many of them are there, Seoras?'

'There'll be at least seven,' he said, 'probably more. I know there'll be down numbers now, having finished off another two.'

Macleod could make out a couple of figures in white habits surrounding smaller figures. That was probably where the children were, and he tore off towards them before he saw someone running towards him. Macleod saw a hand raised, assumed there was something in it, and dropped his shoulder, clattering into the approaching monk's habit. They both hit the ground causing a small splash from the sodden earth. Macleod rolled over and over but managed to get a hand on his attacker's wrist. He forced it into the ground several times before he heard something drop with a splash.

'Damn you, Macleod. Damn you. If I can't kill the kids, I'll kill a Christian for him.'

191

Macleod thought it was Forbes, but there was no light, no way to tell except for the voice. Macleod put his hand up on the man's face, driving him back, and rolled over so he was on top of the man instead. He managed to drop an elbow into the man's face, holding him there before he heard Hope crying out. She had been knifed before and this sounded like a grunt of pain from having to use the arm, but he couldn't say for sure.

There was a roar of a car engine and a sweeping beam of headlights lit up the scene before Macleod. A naked woman who had obviously been dancing, was suddenly running around frantically. There were at least another five figures in habits, three of whom were beside a number of children. The kids weren't screaming, so maybe they were drugged. Had they been settled down in some way, because anybody would be screaming as the little green sports car was now piling through the moor, headlights on.

The track had been narrow, very narrow, but it hadn't stopped Clarissa as she piled into two of the monks, sending them spinning off the car. Macleod saw her open the car door, step out, and then she screamed. On the edge of the light from the car, it looked like one of the figures had attacked her, and he saw Ross jumping out of the side of the vehicle.

But he realised he'd been watching the scene for too long and not concentrating on the man beneath him. He felt a knee being raised up into his stomach, and with a grunt Macleod fell off the man, feeling the water soaking through his jacket, and the cold into the back of his neck.

'Damn you, Macleod,' he said. Macleod tried to push at the man. In the dim light from the car headlights, Macleod could see Forbes. He had a knife raised ready to strike down on Macleod. As the man bent over, Macleod kicked up with a leg catching him in the stomach. The knife fell from the man's grasp a second time, but he held himself upright and turned, beginning to run.

Macleod rolled over, helped himself up onto his knees, and ran after Forbes. His feet splashed through the boggy moorland, before suddenly they caught on something and he went straight down, his face hitting cold water. As he got up again, he saw the monk's habit being thrown off in the distance, and he thought someone was beside him. Just across, he heard a scream from Hope and saw a man in a habit pulling her arm, twisting the one that had been knifed. Macleod turned, ploughed towards the man, hit him with everything he had just underneath the shoulder.

As the man fell to the ground, Macleod tried to fall onto him, but the man was too strong. Coming upright on his knees, Macleod flung an arm around the man's neck trying to hold him tight, but the man drove his head backwards, butting Macleod, and Macleod could feel his nose being smashed and blood starting to pour.

He was woozy, struggling to maintain his focus when he saw in front of him in the shadows a woman with red hair. Hope drove a punch down into the man's face, one, two, three, four times. The man could barely keep upright on his knees. Macleod wasn't sure if he'd been knocked out cold as Hope continued.

'That's enough,' said Macleod. 'Get the cuffs on him. Get the cuffs on him.' Macleod left Hope with the man and stood up, still woozy, and stumbled over towards the little green sports car.

He saw a man lying on the ground, unsure what condition he was in. Ross was with Clarissa while a number of children wandered around, almost as if nothing was happening.

'She's been knifed,' said Ross. 'It's in the gut.'

Macleod fumbled into his pocket. There had to be a signal. He could see more cars out on the road, and he switched on the light with the phone, tapping it on and off. Three quick flashes, three long flashes, then three quick flashes. A car started coming towards them down the track. Then it stopped and people began running out.

'Stay with her, Ross,' said Macleod, 'get her help.' Hope appeared beside Macleod.

'Have we got them all?' she asked.

'Forbes went that way towards the water.' Macleod looked into the distance. He could still make out a white habit. Hope took him by the arm.

'Come on, Seoras. Come on.'

Macleod stumbled as best he could, still woozy from the butt to the head, but he forced himself on, foot after foot. He saw Hope running with one arm almost strapped to her side while the other arm pumped like she normally did when running. They raced to the edge of the water where they saw an abandoned monk's habit some fifty metres away in the water. They heard splashing and he looked out as best he could out. There was a head there, arms on the move.

'We need to get them,' said Hope, 'they need to pay.'

'You're in no condition to swim,' said Macleod, taking off his coat. He kicked his shoes off, stripped his tie away, and opened the top of his shirt. Almost without thinking, he strode into the water.

In his day, he'd been a good swimmer, but it had been a long time. The first thing that hit him was the cold. He was still only at waist height, and he heard Hope calling after him, but she was right. He needed to get them; he needed to. Without thinking, his legs were moving, and soon the water was up around his neck. It wasn't that bad. It was okay. He could handle this. He let his legs float behind him, began to kick, and tried to swim. As he got further out into the darkness, heading to what he thought were two figures swimming away, Macleod felt like he was seizing up. The water was suddenly colder. The water was . . . he couldn't, he couldn't move his legs properly. He was starting to sink. He felt like his head was fried, his brain not knowing what to do. He reached down with his feet, but he was too far out. There was no bottom here. There was no . . .

Quickly, he pushed up, brought himself to the surface, and tried to gulp some air. He almost choked on it as he descended back through the water with his mouth open. Macleod thrashed out, hands going this way and that, desperately trying to rise up, but his actions were pitiful, causing more problems than they were solving. He felt the panic rush through him. This was not how he'd been when in the cellar, not how he'd been when having to reach up and breathe, but there were steps there. He wasn't swimming that time; he wasn't cold like this.

An arm swept around him, and he felt himself being pulled through the water. Soon his head broke the surface. He gasped, choking. The water was still in his throat. It felt like an age as he was pulled, eventually, out onto the wet ground.

'What are you doing?' cried Hope.

Macleod saw her face above him as torches began to be shone on him. 'What are you doing?' The face above him was pale. It looked bedraggled and exhausted, and the red hair had come out of the ponytail and was dripping all around her face.

'Did we get them?' blurted Macleod.

'No,' said Hope, and there were tears in her eyes. 'I got you. I got you, Seoras. To hell with them.'

Chapter 25

Macleod insisted that he didn't need to go to hospital, but the paramedics were just as insistent back.

'I can take this,' said Hope. 'I can do the sweep-up. It's not a problem.'

'We need to get them. I think that was Forbes and Whitelaw. We need to make sure we get them. They have to be held accountable.'

'Seoras, they went out into the loch. You can't just go swimming into the middle of a loch. It gets colder as you go out. That's what happened to you. You're just lucky I was able to get you.'

'I told you not to go in because of your arm.'

'Well, in fairness, it got a workout for you. Thank you for that. It's much appreciated.'

Macleod smiled briefly. 'I just wanted them, I just wanted them to be held up for it.'

'We got the kids though,' said Hope.

She watched as a Coastguard helicopter lifted up into the night. It disappeared over the horizon, but Macleod could see another one on scene. Its powerful searchlight was sweeping across the loch here and there. He recognised the search parties from the Coastguard as well as well as Mountain Rescue and various police teams. The fire brigade was also there, a massed search party being sent out.

They also wanted people to help comb the ground for there were many knives about. Jona was insistent when she arrived that everyone stay out of her way. Several people had been captured, two of whom were in hospital. Apparently, a car had hit them. He hadn't had time to ask Clarissa about that before she was flown away, for Macleod had sat in the back of the ambulance wrapped up tight, warming up.

'Is Ross okay?' asked Macleod.

'Ross is fine. Not a scratch on him. I think he was more terrified when Clarissa took the car onto the moorland.'

'It didn't look a wide enough track. I thought our car would get bogged down. That's why I ran down.'

'That's what I thought as well. That car of hers is smaller, it's lighter, though I think they're going to need a tractor to get it back out.'

'Well, they better take care of it,' said Macleod laughing. 'She is all right, isn't she?'

'I hope so. I didn't get a chance to see her go. Ross was looking after her. Somebody had to look after you and then organise everyone else.'

'There's something else though. They killed their own people, Hope.'

'Not necessarily. Some of Jona's team said that those that died may have killed themselves. Those last two anyway. The bomb as well. He knew that was coming. He tempted Clarissa in, but we got them,' said Hope. 'Now you need to go and have a quiet night in the hospital. The assistant chief constable's coming down to give me a hand anyway. If Forbes is out there, we'll find him.'

'Have you told . . .'

'Not yet, but I will do. I'll make sure she's down to you.'

'You should wait till morning before telling her. I won't have a night's sleep otherwise.'

'She's watched you go through this,' says Hope. 'Given that, I think the woman deserves to come and pay you a bit of attention. You know it's what she wants to do.'

Macleod nodded. 'Call Jane. You tell her they only do beds for one. She'll know I'm in good form then.'

Macleod sat back in the ambulance and was monitored by the paramedic who sat beside him as the ambulance pulled away from Loch Garry. They were headed for Inverness Hospital, but Macleod closed his eyes and soon drifted off to sleep.

* * *

When Macleod opened his eyes, he was in a small white room on his own, but he could hear a voice outside that he knew. It took about ten minutes before she opened the door and he saw Jane staring at him. He gave a wry smile, and she ran over, throwing her arms around him.

'You're all right then,' she said.

'Yes.' He said. 'I'm fine.'

'You broke your nose.'

He'd almost forgotten about that. He'd struggled so much with the water and the cold, it was like the pain of the nose had just gone away.

'It probably looks worse than it is. I don't feel much.'

199

'It's off to the one side. Don't know if that'll come back,' said Jane. 'You never had your nose broke before in this business?'

'I used to be lively on my feet.'

'I thought you were having armed escorts to help.'

'Who told you that?'

'Jim dropped the odd word. He did keep me informed about what was going on to a point. Well, actually, he told me all the good things like the armed escorts and that. He didn't tell me what you were up to. Certainly, didn't mention any broken noses.'

'In Jim's defence,' said Macleod, 'this was last night. We got them last night though. We got our seven kids, but two of the perpetrators may have got away. We don't know.'

'He said the Coastguard's been out all night along with the fire service, Mountain Rescue, trying to search that loch. Helicopter's been going up and down it. They haven't reported anybody being found.'

Macleod leaned back in the bed and Jane took his hand. 'They put that mural on TV,' she said. 'It all looked very . . . what's the word? Cultic.'

'Occult,' said Macleod quietly. 'It was Satanism.'

She squeezed his hand tight. 'Are you okay?'

'I will be.'

'Was personal, wasn't it?' she said. 'This has been personal to you. Don't deny it. I can tell. You can't hide much from me, Seoras Macleod.'

'You try to stay professional,' he said, 'but this time, well . . . ' He didn't say anything more and she just smiled at him.

'Whenever you're ready, or you can tell that other woman.'

'Clarissa?' he said.

'No, Hope. Just make sure you tell one of us.' Macleod bent

forward, took her head in his hands and kissed her on the forehead.

'I'm not a three-year-old child,' said Jane, and she dove forward, kissing him on the lips.

The impulsiveness always excited him. *It was one of the best things about her*, he thought.

As he left the hospital insisting that he was fine, well before the doctors agreed with him, Macleod asked Jane where she had parked the car. She said that Jim was going to pick them up. He had dropped her off earlier on and said it was probably best if he picked them up. Macleod didn't understand, but as he walked to the front of the hospital, he began to understand why. On either side of the entrance, and kept outside of the actual building, he saw two rows of people as he walked down the corridor towards the front door. He saw nursing staff and doctors turn and applaud him. He put his hands up to say no, but they continued anyway. As he got to the front door, Jim walked in, put out his hand, and shook Macleod's.

'Well done, Seoras. Well done.'

'Did you get them? Did we get them?' asked Macleod.

'We believe the cold water of the loch got them first. I don't think they're coming back. We've got the rest of them. I hear Clarissa got a couple of them with her car.'

'You make sure that comes out unscratched. You can pay for the touch-up job on it if needs be. How is she?'

'Stable. She lost quite a bit of blood. There's no point going to see her at the moment. She's not awake. I was planning on going up and seeing her later this afternoon. Hope sent Ross up earlier on to look in on her. Your sergeant's covering everything off.'

'She's well capable,' said Macleod. 'I hear Lawson was trying to put her up for DI.'

'Would you?' asked Jim suddenly.

Macleod didn't even flinch. 'Straight away,' he said. 'Straight away.'

'Good,' said Jim. 'We'll need a new DCI and you need to think about that.'

Macleod shrugged his shoulders. 'I'd have to talk it over with the boss here.'

'No work talk,' said Jane. 'There's a load of people standing out there desperate to give you a round of applause or something. Can we get out so they can all go home?'

Macleod kept his head down but lifted the occasional hand of thanks. He'd never been applauded before in his life, but this time the media were there in full force, and, thankfully so, were the public.

* * *

Two weeks later in a hotel in Aviemore, Macleod stood up with a glass of Cola, looking around at his team. Clarissa was there in a wheelchair having had a few more difficulties than they'd imagined. She was going to be okay; that was for certain, but the woman looked jaded. Less the dynamic, if somewhat strange, purple-haired Rottweiler, or more like a lost soul. She'd been thanked greatly, especially by the assistant chief constable.

As Macleod beamed around, first at the tech team, and then the constables who had helped his own core unit, he felt immensely proud, but he also realised that some of the people in front of him were hurting. After they'd had their meal and some toasts from the Assistant Chief Constable, the team started talking.

Jane had kissed Macleod on the cheek as he sat with Clarissa and said he could be up as late as he wanted, but she was going to sleep. She understood him, understood that this was when they would talk work. Work was something he didn't want to share fully with her. He also understood that it wasn't something she wanted to share fully with him. Certainly, not the darker sides, but he knew she would if she had to.

Macleod sat beside Clarissa while the others mingled and talked. She looked pale and he put his hand on hers.

'Don't,' she said. 'Don't treat me like some sort of invalid.'

'Because it hurts your pride?' asked Macleod. 'You took a hit. You took a really bad hit this time.'

She nodded. 'How do you do it?' asked Clarissa. 'Because I don't know if I can anymore. This time, I nearly lost it on several occasions, and nearly went too far. All I could see were those kids. The other murders we've handled; they're not pleasant, never something you enjoy, but this wasn't the same.'

'But you saved them. You saved them with that little green sports car,' said Macleod, smiling.

'It was there in the hospital car park when the Assistant Chief Constable brought me out. He drove me home in it. I might not be driving it for a while though. He cleaned up a few dents that were there before as well. That was a bargain.'

Macleod laughed, but he felt her squeeze his hand tightly. 'How do you do it, Seoras? How do you keep going when it's like this?'

He nodded over towards Hope who was chatting with Ross. 'They help,' he said, 'but the wins help too. We've had some losses on the way. I'm not sure if I could have stopped any of them, but there's seven kids alive today because of us. You'll always carry your injuries, but you have to carry your trophies too.'

'I might not be here next time,' said Clarissa. 'I just don't know. I don't know if I can handle this cost. Not just the physical, but the mental this time.'

'If it wasn't for you, we wouldn't have got there when we chased the knives initially with Abby. Integral part of the team.'

'But no one's irreplaceable,' said Clarissa. 'I replaced some-one else. One day, someone will replace me.'

'Hope's probably going to move up to DI,' said Macleod.

'Is she moving on then? Are you moving?'

'I might be moving up,' he said. 'I don't know; it's times like these when you have to think about it. It will all stop one day.'

'When?' said Clarissa. 'When the pain gets too much. When you've taken too much out of yourself to ever live normally after it because that's what it feels like. Antiques wasn't like this.'

'No, I guess it wasn't,' he said, 'but then again, you have to learn to pay it later. Learn to pay it off whatever way you do with whoever you do it with.'

'That's why it's good you've got Jane.' Macleod just nodded.

Three hours later, Macleod was stood on the balcony, looking out to the Cairngorms in what was actually a cold but crisp night. The moon was out, giving a breath-taking view off the back of the hotel. Everyone else had gone, Ross believing he was the last one to go, but Hope had only stepped outside. She deliberately hadn't gone to her room.

'They did well,' said Macleod, 'but Clarissa's struggling.'

'It's understandable,' said Hope. 'There's too much wrong with that case. Too often where we nearly lost it. Too much where everything nearly fell apart. Public eye too—lots of pressure.'

'And you want a DI job,' said Macleod.

'I was hoping that my DCI would be a little bit more reasonable. At least with you, I know I won't be that little trophy on the side, a good-looking woman that can do it for the press.'

He gave a shake of his head. 'Lawson played us,' he said. 'He played us good. He put me in a place I didn't want to be.'

Both of them fell silent. Hope moved across, putting a hand on his shoulder. She felt him tilt his head in towards her, resting his head on her shoulder, or rather just below it because she was too tall for him to be able to do that. Suddenly he was shaking, and she put a second arm around him, pulling him close, almost like a baby.

'Gleary. I had to go to Gleary, Hope. With all that that guy's done, I watched him threaten his niece. He tore her apart. He tore her apart and I couldn't do anything about it. All for an address, all for . . . '

'You did what you had to do,' said Hope. 'You did what you had to do for seven little kids.'

'Did I? Did I do what I had to do? With this faith of mine, you're told to trust, and this was a test of faith. Was it not? Good versus evil in a proper sense.'

'It's always good versus evil,' said Hope. 'Isn't it?'

'I don't know,' said Macleod. She could feel him sniffing at first and then actually crying. She wrapped her arms around him, pulled him close, and her hair fell around his head. He could feel it touching his ears, and he wept. As she held him, he could hear her beginning to cry, too.

'Nearly lost you, Seoras,' she said through choked tears. 'We nearly lost all of us.'

For a moment, they continued to cry and then they straightened up. He looked out into the distance at the silvery moon falling on the mountainous landscape around him. Then he turned and smiled at his friend and colleague beside him. She looked unusual because her hair was down, something she never did while actually on duty.

'Before you take DI, make sure you're wanting to do it. Each time you go up, the cost gets greater.'

Hope put her finger up to Macleod's mouth. 'Quiet. They always say you and I are not alike. I'm a six-foot redhead who looks great in her leather jacket and jeans.' Hope smiled, almost laughing. 'You're an old fart, running around in a suit, tie, and raincoat and probably less action and more thought, but you and I are the same. This is what we do. This is who we are, and we'll always pay the cost for it. Don't even pretend to me you're not taking the job. Jane will never stand in your way.'

She reached forward and kissed him on the forehead. 'I'm looking forward to working with my new DCI,' she said.

Hope strolled off to the door of the balcony and was about to go through when she stopped and looked back. 'Of course, it'll be a far better-looking DI they're going to have now at the station.'

Macleod laughed, and then he turned back to look out at the mountainside. He thought he heard something. Somebody was coming close. For a moment he hesitated, and then felt the arms slip around his waist and pull him close.

'She's right, you know. The two of you are very alike. Coppers till you die. Just don't die on me, Seoras.' Jane buried her face into his back.

Read on to discover the Patrick Smythe series!

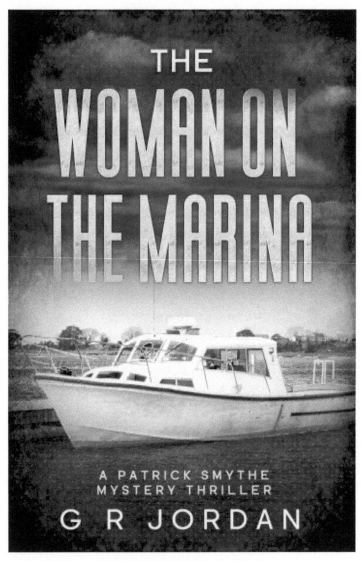

Start your Patrick Smythe journey here!

Patrick Smythe is a former Northern Irish policeman who

after suffering an amputation after a bomb blast, takes to the sea between the west coast of Scotland and his homeland to ply his trade as a private investigator. Join Paddy as he tries to work to his own ethics while knowing how to bend the rules he once enforced. Working from his beloved motorboat 'Craigantlet', Paddy decides to rescue a drug mule in this short story from the pen of G R Jordan.

Join G R Jordan's monthly newsletter about forthcoming releases and special writings for his tribe of avid readers and then receive your free Patrick Smythe short story.

Go to https://bit.ly/PatrickSmythe for your Patrick Smythe journey to start!

About the Author

GR Jordan is a self-published author who finally decided at forty that in order to have an enjoyable lifestyle, his creative beast within would have to be unleashed. His books mirror that conflict in life where acts of decency contend with self-promotion, goodness stares in horror at evil, and kindness blindsides us when we at our worst. Corrupting our world with his parade of wondrous and horrific characters, he highlights everyday tensions with fresh eyes whilst taking his methodical, intelligent mainstays on a roller-coaster ride of dilemmas, all the while suffering the banter of their provoca-tive sidekicks.

A graduate of Loughborough University where he masquer-aded as a chemical engineer but ultimately played American football, Gary had worked at changing the shape of cereal flakes and pulled a pallet truck for a living. Watching vegeta-bles freeze at -40'C was another career highlight and he was also one of the Scottish Highlands "blind" air traffic controllers.

These days he has graduated to answering a telephone to people in trouble before telephoning other people to sort it out.

Having flirted with most places in the UK, he is now based in the Isle of Lewis in Scotland where his free time is spent between raising a young family with his wife, writing, figuring out how to work a loom and caring for a small flock of chickens. Luckily, his writing is influenced by his varied work and life experience as the chickens have not been the poetical inspiration he had hoped for!

You can connect with me on:

🌐 https://grjordan.com

📘 https://facebook.com/carpetlessleprechaun

Subscribe to my newsletter:

✉ https://bit.ly/PatrickSmythe

Also by G R Jordan

G R Jordan writes across multiple genres including crime, dark and action adventure fantasy, feel good fantasy, mystery thriller and horror fantasy. Below is a selection of his work. Whilst all books are available across online stores, signed copies are available at his personal shop.

Dormie 5 (Highlands and Islands Detective Thrillers #25)
A clash of cultures at a golf club of distinction. The club secretary found sliced on the 15th tee box. Can Macleod and McGrath find the rogue player on the course before some else receives a two slash penalty?

With the building of the new parkland course beside Newton-moray's famous old links, tensions rise in the realms of the club's devoted golfers. But when there is talk of a professional tour event coming to the club and being switched to the new course, the gloves are off in a fight for the event. In the midst of the fervour, the club secretary is found dead over his golf trolley at the picturesque 15th hole. Can Seoras and Hope wade through the club politics and personalities to uncover a brutal killer, or will the clubhouse row lead to more patrons being teed up!

The match might be dormie, but they'll play to the death!

A Personal Favour (A Kirsten Stewart Thriller #9)
A friend's daughter goes missing when reporting for a local paper. A town on the up but with a history steeped in blood. Can Kirsten break the steely cocoon of silence and find the girl before she is another tragic story?

Dealing with the desperate change in their circumstances, Craig receives a plea from an old friend to find his missing daughter. Being in no shape to assist, Kirsten takes his place and finds herself in a cold wilderness that lacks a warm welcome. When she digs too deep into the past, a desperate town seals itself off, leaving Kirsten trapped within.

Some stories are just too personal for the public to hear!

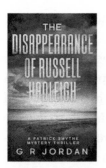

The Disappearance of Russell Hadleigh (Patrick Smythe Book 1)

https://grjordan.com/product/the-disappearance-of-russell-hadleigh

retired judge fails to meet his golf partner. His wife calls for help while running a fantasy play ring. When Russians start co-opting into a fairly-traded clothing brand, can Paddy untangle the strands before the bodies start littering the golf course?

In his first full novel, Patrick Smythe, the single-armed former policeman, must infiltrate the golfing social scene to discover the fate of his client's husband. Assisted by a young starlet of the greens, Paddy tries to understand just who bears a grudge and who likes to play in the rough, culminating in a high stakes showdown where lives are hanging by the reaction of a moment. If you love pacey action, suspicious motives and devious characters, then Paddy Smythe operates amongst your kind of people.

Love is a matter of taste but money always demands more of its suitor.

Lightning Source UK Ltd.
Milton Keynes UK
UKHW011959120123
415233UK00001B/172